Rooted Wings

&

Phantom Wolf

Eternal Soul Mate Trilogy

I0599624

By

Leah Silverwhisp

Rooted Wings & Phantom Wolf

ISBN: 979-8-9990173-1-4

Leah Silverwhisp

ACKNOWLEDGMENTS

I had so much fun writing *Rooted Wings & Phantom Wolf*, but I couldn't have done it without my lovely support team. First and foremost, a huge thank you to my friends and classmates in the Spicy Librarian club, Sara and Crystal, my two spice experts. Thank you both for your encouragement, advice, and feedback throughout the writing process. Without the two of you, I wouldn't have the confidence to publish my book.

Special thanks to my best friend Aster, who not only encouraged me to write the book but to continue writing afterwards, for he saw me at my best when I was writing. He also encouraged me to take breaks and get some rest too. Thank you for always looking after me, when I get too lost. You pull me back.

Now, to the one who inspired this book. I do not know who you are or what you are up to. I could imagine a million different ways and never get it exactly right, but still you inspired me. You inspired me to hope, to believe, to keep chasing my dreams, and grow. Thank you for the inspiration.

Lastly, a huge warm thank you to those of you who give *Rooted Wings & Phantom Wolf* a chance. I had so much fun writing this book and exploring the characters. I hope you enjoyed exploring the love connection between Haili and Shev.

Leah Silverwhisp

ABOUT THE AUTHOR

Leah Silverwhisp is a romantic at heart and a firm believer that a little magic makes everything better. Her debut novel blends modern-day romance with a pinch of fantasy, a lot of laughter, and just enough awkward charm to feel like real life—if real life had more dragons and spontaneous spells.

She holds a BA in English and has received several honors over the years, including membership in the National Society of Leadership and Success. When not writing, Leah spends her time reading everything she can get her hands on, doodling her daydreams into sketchbooks, and lovingly obsessing over dragons (the winged, fire-breathing kind—though she'd happily adopt a small one if given the chance).

Leah writes to make people laugh, swoon, and believe in happy endings—with a few magical detours along the way.

DEDICATION

For my fellow spicy librarians and the ones who have yet to find
their special someone, I hope you enjoy
Rooted Wings & Phantom Wolf.

Leah Silverwhisp

Table of Contents

Leah Silverwhisp

Content Warning

Reader's discretion be advised — this book bites in the best way with some stalking and bondage play in mind.

Shevaron: Prologue

Another grueling day of pack lessons.

My father insisted I needed to "toughen up" if I was going to take on the Alpha role one day, but deep down, I wasn't sure I even wanted it. Not yet. Not like this. I was only twenty-three. I had plans—real ones—with Owen. Travel the world, explore ancient ruins, chase forgotten myths and lost magick, not protocols and hierarchy.

Uncle Will stood by the fire pit, his voice steady but familiar as he launched into another lecture about asserting dominance and commanding respect. The fire crackled beside us, the scent of pine and charred wood hanging thick in the air. I half listened, half drifted—just enough to keep from getting called out. Uncle Will never pressed hard, not like my father. He knew I was smart. Knew I was searching.

He also knew I felt trapped.

And then, the howl.

One long, ragged note that cut through the forest like a blade.

9

Uncle Will froze. His eyes, sharp and weathered from decades of battles, turned deadly serious. Then—chaos. Snarls and growls erupted from the trees, shadowy shapes darting between trunks. I could barely track them before they descended upon us. Rogue wolves. Fast, feral, coordinated.

Uncle Will moved first, shielding me. He barked a single command—"Run!"—before he launched himself into the fray. I hesitated. I wanted to fight. I wanted to help. But I wasn't ready. My body hadn't shifted yet. I was still human. Vulnerable. Weak.

And then—pain. A sharp, splitting heat bloomed through my bones, spreading like fire. My legs buckled. My chest caved. Snap. Crack. Pop! The world blurred as my body turned inside out. Bones broke and reformed. Skin split and sealed again. Every nerve screamed.

I fell to the forest floor, writhing in agony. My first shift. It was never supposed to happen like this. Not in fear. Not in blood.

Leah Silverwhisp

But survival has a way of overriding destiny.

Rogue wolves lunged for me, but I was no longer prey. Instinct surged forward, violent and primal. I moved before I even knew how. One swipe. A snap of teeth. A howl that wasn't mine, not fully. I tore through them with everything I had, blood soaking the dirt beneath my paws.

I had one thought—my parents. I had to get to them.

I ran, faster than I'd ever moved, half-shifted and bloodied, the scent of smoke and wet earth trailing me. By the time I reached the manor, the estate grounds were littered with the aftermath of battle.

And then I saw them.

My father—Alpha—was dead.

My mother—barely breathing, broken and bruised.

And standing above her was the rogue Alpha, eyes gleaming with mockery, teeth stained red.

Leah Silverwhisp

I should have been afraid. I wasn't. I was already gone, already drowning in fury and pain. But then—something changed.

A whisper.

A warmth.

Not physical, but deep. Soul-deep.

'I feel like I should write something profound, but all I can say is that if you are out there and this somehow gets through to you, then I have only one thing to tell you. Good luck and don't do anything that you will regret later.'

A voice. A soul I'd never heard before and yet somehow always known.

Her.

Haili.

Her words slowed the spiral. Anchored me. Pulled me back from the edge of bloodlust and revenge. I breathed. I felt. I chose.

And I fought—clear-eyed, deliberate, in control. I called for help. Owen and the others came. Together, we took down the rogue Alpha. Together, we survived.

But that was the day everything changed.

That was the day I shifted.

The day I lost my father.

The day I became Alpha.

And the day I first heard her.

Leah Silverwhisp

Haili: Unexpected Visitor

Something about the word *soon* echoes in the back of my mind. It whispers through the doors of my soul as if tempting me to hope for things that have yet to happen. Maybe—just maybe—there's someone out there for me too. However, that kind of hope can be maddening if not managed properly. I think this as I pour over one of my many dense textbooks that deal with word formulas and overexplained definitions that can also drive anyone mad from staring at the page for too long. Yet the word *soon* nips at my soul expecting me to play its game.

Flipping to the next page, I kick my feet in the air as I lie on my bed. The word *formulas* stares back at me, and I let out a deep sigh, tapping my fingers on the page. "How soon is soon," I find myself asking out loud. Dare I entertain this game and allow myself to embrace this unknown soon?

My focus starts to wane away from the textbook. *Soon.* The word echoes in the back of my mind. "Nope. Not going down that

Leah Silverwhisp

rabbit hole," I mutter to myself, shaking off the thought. I push through the rest of the chapter, finishing the exercises displayed on my laptop.

Rolling onto my side, I grab my purple earbuds and slip them into my ears. I press play on my phone, letting the familiar rhythm of an audiobook fill my mind. It's a dark romance—one of my guilty pleasures. I lean back, checking off boxes in my head about what kind of kinks I might have, and others don't. Have that primal prey and predator kink mixed up with the brat kink. At least, I think I do. Whenever the main female character gets bratty with the male and ends off being chased playfully or if she gets treated like a game to win. The challenge of wanting to win and lose at the same time, something about it gets me super wet with arousal and sexually frustrated as hell.

I slowly shift around in my bed pressing my head against the pillow as I try to shut my brain off from even entertaining this idea of hope. *Focus on the book*, I tell myself. I listen to the witty banter between the two

15

main characters that always hooks me in. I think I have listened to this audiobook about five times now. I can't help but admire the balance of teasing and affection, the push and pull of two strong personalities. Maybe I just enjoy the challenge it represents. After all, ordinary relationships don't seem to work for me. I've tried twice, both with a two-timing cheater, and after that, it never happened again. Hey, at least I got a story out it. I can honestly say I lost my virginity inside of a Christian cult compound that the guy worked for and lived in their apartment. Though it honestly felt like a cheap hotel room, and what I assume was missionary style as I laid on my back with him on top as he moved inside of me had done nothing for me.

I pause the audiobook and glance over at my oracle deck sitting on the desk. *Do I?* My best friend Ash and I had a long talk recently about relationships and whether the right person might appear when I least expect it. Curiosity tempts me to seek out the answers I already know. I crawl across the bed, grab the deck, and shuffle it. With a

16

deep breath, I draw a single card:
Unexpected Visitors.

I stare at the card, its meaning sinking in. The last time I pulled this card, Ash showed up out of nowhere during a rough patch with my sister and whisked me away for an impromptu adventure. "Expect the unexpected," I murmur. Could Ash and I have manifested something—or someone— without realizing it?

The cards seem to say yes.

I groan as I put my deck away. Seriously? I don't know what to do with this hope.

*

The next day, I head to work and start running shoes. My focus is on helping customers and making sure everything else is in order while my co-workers slack off or attend to their own departments. I focus on the work I need to do until something ignites in my soul, something more dangerous than hope. A question of the sanity. A teasing voice in the back of my mind about the books I have been reading. His growly voice

17

about him claiming me and edging me to oblivion.

Focus, I tell myself as I laser line the shoes along the shelves. *You are at work and now is not the time to*, he interrupts my thoughts with a chuckle that ignites my soul even more. My face flushes, knowing all too well that my sanity is perfectly fine, and he just enjoys my reactions. I pull another shoe box in line with the others.

Shev, I think to myself as if I were responding to him. *You are doing this on purpose.*

Am I? Shev chuckles in the back of my head, and as if he could lean in close and whisper in my ear, *Maybe I just enjoy watching and listening to your reactions.*

You know most people would just do this to me in person, I grumble in my thoughts. An image flashes in my mind of me not only reacting to him but losing my composure completely. Most people don't believe in the supernatural or magick of the souls and would surely question my sanity if I told them I was having this conversation with

Leah Silverwhisp

him. However, those that mirror me, who walk among the supernatural and often play with magick of the soul among other things know better. I can say for a fact I have not lost my sanity. Though my mundane life says otherwise.

I'm not most people, darling, Shev teases and I can feel his wolfish grin. *If I were to tease you in person, I would lay siege upon your walls and drag you out of your timid castle.*

Is that a challenge? I say as hope roots itself deep inside of my soul. *Well, love, if you really want to siege my castle and claim me, you'd better be ready to catch me,* I tease back with my own wolfish grin. *Get ready to run, wolf boy; where your game ends, my game begins.*

19

Shevaron:

Pack Mentality

"Oh darling, the game is just getting started," I say to myself as I stand in a living room filled with packed boxes. I knew Haili would be my mate the minute our souls touched each other. The second our souls touched, they ignited like phoenix fire burning away any form of negative thoughts and leaving hope in its wake.

Someone coughs and I look up to see my pack brother Jack come in with the hand truck to load the next set of boxes into the moving truck. I catch him looking over at me as he stands there in just his jeans and sneakers.

"Yes, Jack," I say, tossing him a gray T-shirt from the laundry backet that sat on top of one the boxes. "Stop torturing the girls when we are moving."

"Aren't we moving too soon? The house isn't even built yet. It's still a plot of land,"

Leah Silverwhisp

Jack says, catching the shirt and pulling it over messing up his dark hair a little.

"We need to be in the area, but not at the same time before we move in," I say, thinking about what I am going to do once we arrive in the new home development. How would I tease Haili next, what expression would she give next. I'm dying to see her face in person. I don't just want our souls to touch either, I want to consume all of her and make her entirely mine.

Unfortunately, our paths are forced to linger in our two worlds a bit longer than either of us wants. I live in the world of supernatural, while she lives in the mundane—For now. In her life, Haili has sought higher levels of education, and her family has kept her close between work and friends. Meanwhile, I have my pack and kind of work remotely as a data annotator, pre-screening documents before passing them along to AI. Not the most exciting job in the world, but it pays the bills and allows me to run the pack, while I keep a light soul connection to Haili.

Leah Silverwhisp

"Are you sure she is ready for this, pack life isn't exactly easy, Shev," Jack asks as he shoves the hand truck underneath a stack of boxes.

I heave out a heavy sigh and think about all the chaos the pack goes through from securing hunting grounds to dealing with rogue mutts that anger witches, vampires, and other creatures that hide in plain sight. Once you are a part of the supernatural world, there is no going back. Haili has only grazed the top of it and has not shifted fully yet, but her power is growing stronger with each coming year. Whether Haili is ready or not to fully be a part of our world and live alongside the mundane, she will need the pack for support. To be honest, deep down I know Haili doesn't have that much time left at all. My appearance in her life will of course speed up the process, but the mere thought of her going through her first shift alone unsettles me. Soon her body will break and mend itself repeatedly, it doesn't matter how much pain tolerance she has. Her body will be burning from the inside out of the amount of healing it will have to do and

Leah Silverwhisp

Rooted Wings   &   Phantom Wolf

from somewhere deep inside of her, a primal urge will take over. It will rip and claw its way out as she transforms into a wolf.

I shake my head at Jack. "Haili can handle it. What I am worried about is her handling this alone and her time is fast approaching."

Jack pauses for a moment and raises his eyebrow. "And soul connecting with her and making her question her sanity is like what, a way to keep her distracted from what is about to happen?"

I pick up one of the boxes closest to me and stack it on top of the pile that Jack was about to move. Leaning in close, I let a low rumble escape my throat. "My soul connection with her is not a distraction, Jack. Now move the boxes into the truck."

He immediately goes quiet and resumes moving the boxes into the moving truck out front. I turn around and head into the kitchen that has not been fully packed yet. I pack away the rest of the pots and pans as I think about what my next move is going to be. Sure, I tease her and keep her guessing, while I move behind the scenes and move

23

Leah Silverwhisp

into her neighborhood to keep a close eye on her. But what then, my presence is sure to stir up some kind of trouble especially since Jack and the rest of the pack are going to be coming with me, but not all of us will be in the same house. I put most of the pack right at the end of her street in a far bigger house than the one that is being built right across from her.

She has plenty of time before we officially move in since both houses are still being built and probably won't be ready until maybe mid-September and it's early March now. I tape the box closed shut and hear Jack come back inside to grab the next set of boxes grumbling about how I'm not helping to move the boxes into the truck. Someone has to pack up the kitchen and Jack knows nothing about what's going on inside of a kitchen. It was either me or Owen who cooks for the pack. Jack is an excellent hacker. It didn't take him long to hack into Haili's parents' security cameras, not only to watch her but the house being built as well.

I pull out my cell phone and tap on the app that Jack installed into my phone; a screen pulls up off the front porch and there she is in her baggy sweatshirt and leggings with her hair tied up into a messy ponytail. Haili walks out and down towards the street with a leash in her hand, walking the family schnauzer. She walks down the street towards the end of the street where the pack house is being built. On her way back, I see her stop as she sees *our* house being built. I see her face flush slightly as she turns to look away. Her lips curve into a slight smile. Oh, if I was there in person, I would make those lips mine. That would be the first of many things I would do to her.

Haili goes inside the house with her dog and disappears from my video feed. I wonder if I should ask Jack to hack into her laptop. Though based on how he was behaving, Jack had a moral code and probably wouldn't go beyond the front door. I get out of the application and look up to see not Jack but Owen standing in the doorway with a small grocery bag. Owen is wearing his usual baggy T-shirt and jeans. He strolls into the room and places the bag on the table.

Leah Silverwhisp

"I got us a couple of easy meals for the road," he says as an ice breaker before getting serious. "Jack was wearing one of my shirts, did he lose his again?"

"Yeah, to one of the girls watching us move. I just tossed him a random shirt to put on," I say as I start packing up another box. "I'll replace it if he ends up losing that one too."

"He also seemed to be focused on loading the truck today," Owen casually notes.

I pack away the paper towels, napkins, and silverware into the same box as I listen to Owen's calm, mature voice. "Jack, though very talented at being a hacker, has yet to experience a soul connection and tends to stand out too much especially when girls are around."

"Oh, he has young wolf syndrome," Owen concludes. "He will grow out of it, eventually. What did you say to make him focus on his responsibility on packing up the truck?"

Leah Silverwhisp

"I simply just told him that my soul connection with Haili isn't a distraction and to stop messing around," I answer while taping up another box and labeling it: Kitchen. "I may have intentionally intimidated him when I said it too."

Owen quietly nods and starts to help pack up the boxes. "How long do you think Haili has before it starts happening to her?"

I look up from one of my boxes. "Until her birthday in October. Her birthday, unfortunately, lands on the day when the veil starts to thin and that will cause her powers to grow even more to the point of her probably shifting. The stronger Haili becomes, the more eyes she will attract."

"Right," Owen agrees. "Best to act as unseen bodyguards and build that connection with her. Though, I feel that the game you are making the soul connection between you and Haili is more for you than it is for her."

"Says the wolf who found his mate and decided to make cooking for her into a scavenger hunt," I say teasingly as a goofy

27

Leah Silverwhisp

grin appears on Owen's face. "Maybe, I should ask Selene for her thoughts on the subject."

"You know, I bet she would love that," Owen says as he labels a couple of boxes: Kitchen.

Jack pops his head into the room. "Are you two done yet? I could really use the help especially since the girls keep trying to stop me as I load up the moving truck."

Leah Silverwhisp

Haili: Wolf Spirit

Oh fuck, I must be losing my mind. I keep looking for signs like a love-struck fool. The hopeful romantic side of me keeps checking to see if my soul reacts to anything. That house in front of me tugs at my soul with hints of importance that I have yet to understand. Sure, that house may hold a key to a mystery that I may not understand. Scooby pulls on the leash eager to return home from his walk. "Alright, Scooby, we are going, just stop pulling," I say, breaking away from my thoughts and heading up the driveway before entering the house.

Once inside, I let Scooby loose to roam the house and find my way to my bookshelf. Which book shall distract me today? After all, it's my day off from both school and work. Maybe listening to another audiobook to drown out my thoughts. I search through the bookcase and pick one of my spicy demon books that has to do with revenge. This one would do just nicely. I turn towards my bed and think for a moment how nice it would be to cuddle up someone in my bed and read a book with them. Then a thought about being fucked in the same bed to the point of being unable to think crosses my mind. Yep, definitely losing my mind. No going back, I already let hope in and there I can't take it back. Plus, something tells me that the timing of everything has a specific purpose.

Scooby pads up to me and nuzzles my leg sensing my restlessness as I hold the book in my hand. I look down at him. "I'm okay, Scooby, just wondering if I need to do another card reading to confirm my sanity." I pat his head and place the book down on my desk. Then I pick up one of my decks I got from my travels and give it a shuffle, focusing on the question about the house across the street. I pull the card out and freeze. Wolf Spirit: Family. You got to be fricken kidding me. I put the card down on top of the deck and stroll over to the front window with my eyes locked on the house that now has all of its walls and roof put up. I stare out at it as the workers continue to work on it.

Damn my intuition, what am I supposed to do with this knowledge? The house has now

Leah Silverwhisp

turned into a clock that is ticking down. Though let's be honest here, the clock has been ticking down for quite some time now. I could keep ignoring it. I mean it was easy. Nothing has happened yet, and it probably won't. At least, not immediately. I have always known I am different from my family. I am not just the only witch in the family, but I belong to the supernatural world too. There have been small tells. My keen sense of hearing and smells, the strong soul connection with Shev, and natural strength matched with instincts. I stopped thinking about it ages ago and focused on what I could control such as school and work. I was probably never going to shift, for nothing exciting or thrilling has ever reached my doorstep.

I walk back to my bedroom where Scooby has taken over my desk chair because he is not allowed on my bed. He licks my hand as I pat his head before I grab the demon smut off my desk. "You know, Scooby, I could act like none of this is happening to me and distract myself from it all with books."

Not like dogs could talk, but he is a very good listener. Of course, I don't believe a word of what I am saying. I can't ignore this. There is literally a house involved, a strong soul connection that makes my whole body ache with anticipation, and I'm getting more restless by the day. Maybe that's why I prefer dark rom coms compared to the regular rom coms; the main male characters do whatever it takes to be with the woman they love. I meant it when I told Shev that the minute his game ends, mine begins because he has made me wait.

I sit down on my bed and open to the first page of the book. The words aren't sinking in as I try to read them in my room quietly. Yet, I feel like I should be doing something else. A low rumble from the garage door sounds and I know. Mom's home. I close the book and sigh deeply, time to be social. I leave my room alongside Scooby who is excited to see Mom.

"Hey, Mom," I say as I enter the dining room and kitchen area.

Mom smiles at me and puts down the groceries. "Your sister and the gang are coming over this weekend. Are you ready?"

Nope, I was never ready for that. My whole family sees me as the precious youngest sibling that could do no wrong. Of course, a lot of their actions are out of love, and I get it, I do. They're older, wiser, and don't want me to make the same mistakes that they did. I wasn't going at their pace. I still live with Mom and Dad, but I am going to graduate school online and working a part-time job that doesn't give me enough to live on my own. I still don't have a license, let alone a car to drive and call my own. Yet, I don't need one. I am about to leave work anyway and planning to work remotely after I graduate college. If I want to go out, all I have to do is ask, but right now the gas prices are going up and it's best to save whenever you can. Therefore, I carpool and if I can afford to, I help pay for gas, though if they refuse, I usually offer to pay for lunch or gift them money for one of their hobbies. Yes, I spend a lot of time in my room because it is my sacred space. Inside my room, I am allowed

Leah Silverwhisp

to be myself fully, I'm allowed to be naked and feel safe among my things. I can be Haili the witch, I can be Haili the wolf, the reader, the writer, the gamer or any one number of things I set my mind to. Beyond my bedroom, I am not safe from the side comments – concerns – and words that I care too much about as they stick to me like clear-glue.

"Define ready," I answer as I start thinking about homework and work. "I have to work this weekend and clean up my first draft for one of my classes, while I am waiting to clean my bathroom because it's a bit too soon."

"Haili, you are making a face. What's up?" Mom asks, noticing that my facial expression has changed.

Damnit, I really have no poker face. If I ever get taken in for questioning, I will have to be straight up honest and to the point. "I just have a lot on my plate right now. Nothing to stress over, I am just making sure I have time for the family by making sure I have all my ducks in a row. Between work, school," and the secrets I have been keeping, "and just trying to get back to the roots that make me, me."

"Are you sure, that's all there is?" she asks me, still concerned yet understanding.

"Of course." I give her a smile. "I'm adulting, I can handle it."

"Alright," she says. "Don't worry about the bathroom, I'll take care of it. You just focus on school and work."

"Thanks, Mom," I say, hugging her and then head back to my room.

I close my bedroom door behind me and look at my laptop. Maybe, I should write a little if I can't focus on reading a book right now. My thoughts come to a halt as a single realization washes over me. Restless soul and being compelled to write up a storm right now, could only mean one thing. I sit down at my desk and glance at the black screen I have yet to turn on. Shev inspired and awakened the inner writer in me, which shook everything else up inside of me. I'm going to have to bang out my homework in order to write all of this out of my system or I might actually lose my sanity. Oddly enough, I feel free in this feeling, like I could run away with my writing and read my books, while I study hard for school.

Shevaron:

Driving Pains

On the road, I drive the moving truck down towards South Carolina. Not the ideal place to be, but you know what they say: "If you want something, go get it." I'll *make it work*; I smirked to myself. One of Haili's mantras that has rubbed off on me since I spied on her through soul connections. If Jack only knew that soul connecting with your mate is considered the ultimate hack. I have a direct connection to Haili. She cannot hide from me. I long to see her big, beautiful blue eyes with her thin eyebrows express themselves in a way when she realizes her walls mean nothing to me.

Owen changes the radio station as "There's Nothing Holding Me Back" by Shawn Mendes starts to play pulling me out of my thoughts. "Selene loves this song. She makes me sing and dance to this with her."

"Please tell me there's a video of this," I tease. "I need Selene to send it to me."

Leah Silverwhisp

"Unfortunately for you, the videos that do exist are considered pornographic," Owen says with a wolfish grin. "Plus, I'm not even allowed to watch them. They are only for Selene to enjoy."

I chuckle to myself as I drive. "Yeah, that does sound like something that Selene would do. I see why you put her in charge of Jack."

"He will be missed," Owen says evilly.

Owen and Selene really do complement each other. Both are brilliant evil masterminds with hearts of gold. Jack stands no chance with them; he is probably stuck in the car with Selene as she listens to her favorite Disney villain songs or one of her audiobooks. Either way, he is doomed. On cue, Owen's phone buzzes as the name: The Shirtless One appears on his phone with a picture of Jack being shirtless.

"Put it on speaker," I say as I continue to be mindful of the road.

Owen answers the phone and puts it on speaker, "Still alive?"

"I'm begging you, switch cars with me. Ride with your mate and the rest of the pack," Jack's voice comes through over the phone as "Into the Dark of the Night" plays in the background with multiple voices of pack members singing along to it. "She got the whole pack singing along with her."

I feel a devilish smile come across my face. "Sorry, Jack, but if anyone is switching, it would be Owen and Selene. I need at least one of them with the rest of the pack."

Owen snickers next to me. "I could switch with Selene, if you are truly suffering, Jack. Would you like me to switch with my wife?"

I focus on the road, knowing what would happen if Owen switched with Selene. I can only imagine what Owen has planned in that diabolical head of his. I wonder if the two of them planned this in advance to mess with Jack. I switch lanes and think to myself as Jack struggles with whether to trust Owen or not with his offer.

"Listen, Jack, once we reach Virginia, I'll have Owen switch and take over driving the

39

pack, so Selene can rest up in the moving van. Until then you must endure," I say as if I was trying to help him out.

"Or I could switch with you and Owen can drive the moving truck and you ride with the pack," Jack responds, the singing in the background getting louder. "Help me!"

"Unfortunately for you, the moving truck is under my name, so I must be the one driving it," I say innocently with a smirk.

"I'll see you in Virginia, Owen," Jack says before releasing a heavy sigh. "If I lose my mind before then, I blame you, Shev."

Owen ends the call and laughs out loud; he so had planned the switch with Selene. And I am their willing accomplice. "So, how are you going to torture Jack?" I ask as I watch the cars around me switch lanes.

"Selene and I made a specific CD for this occasion," Owen says, not giving too much away.

A couple of hours later, I pull into a truck stop with the pack and as everyone gets out to stretch their legs, I see Selene stretch out

40

Leah Silverwhisp

her arms acting sleepy as she asks Owen to get her some snacks from the convenience store inside. She has her blonde hair braided up in the fishtail style, and is wearing leggings with a crimson baggy T-shirt she probably stole from Owen. She strolls over to the moving truck and leans up against the passenger door fake-yawning. She looks over at me with a playful smile.

"So, how does it feel to be closer to your girl even from this distance," she asks teasingly.

I lean up against the truck beside her. "Suspenseful, so close, yet so far," I say, and it takes every ounce of strength not to rush things. If I wasn't doing this the right way, I would hop into the moving truck and drive straight to Haili. I would scoop her up in my arms and kiss her lips, before stealing her away from the world she knows. I would reawaken her to everything all in one night. I would make her mine and claim every inch of her body. Unfortunately, I can't do that. At least not yet. Haili needs time to finish up school and enjoy her mundane life without

41

Leah Silverwhisp

worry just a little longer. If I move too fast, that time will be taken away from her.

"Yeah, that was how it felt with Owen. Though I think it was more torture for him than it was for me," she says as we watch him and the pack exit the convenience store with a bunch of snacks.

"He sent you on a scavenger hunt," I say, watching Owen instruct the pack members to get back to Selene's forest-green SUV.

"I'll let you in on a little secret Shev," Selene says as Owen gets into the driver's seat of her car. "In the game between mates, the real game begins when the script becomes flipped," she teases before walking away from the truck and over to the SUV to claim her snacks before Owen eats them all on her.

Haili's words echo in the back of my mind, *when your game ends, my game begins.* She has a game too. So, that must mean that Owen had to play Selene's game. What was her game? You know what, I don't want to know. I'll just take her for her word that Owen was tortured more than her. I walk

Leah Silverwhisp

over to the driver's side of the moving truck and hop in. Moments later, Selene slides into the passenger seat and closes the door. I pull the moving truck out of the truck stop and get back on track to South Carolina.

Once everyone gets back on the road, I hear Selene count with her fingers. "Three – Two – One," her phone rings with same nametag and picture that Owen has for Jack in his phone. She answers it, "Hello, Jack, thank you for your request to switch. Now, I can nap with ease." She puts the phone call on the speaker option so I could hear his response.

"You—," a slight pause in his voice. "You planned this, didn't you? You made this CD specifically to torture me. Whose idea was it?"

Selene just giggles and hangs up the phone. "That would be Owen's idea actually," she confesses to me and to no one else. "I just chose the music, recorded it, and drove Jack nuts. Owen was the one that bribed the rest of the pack to go along with it."

43

Leah Silverwhisp

Haili: Maple Spirit

How many days has it been since I started writing, almost a week? Yeah, it has been almost a week of compulsively writing down everything. Poems, short stories, a random novel, and even lyrics that I for one will not be singing to anyone. Unless they want to hear me butcher the beautiful lyrics. Better not try. I haven't soul-connected conversed with Shev in a while. It is only when he wants to, but when I want to, nothing. One-way communication, which gives me plenty of time to figure out how I am going to work this. Yes, I have school and work down flat. So, that leaves plenty of time to plot a game of my own. After all, I am a writer, and I can make anything work. However, our whole soul connection thing we have going on here means that he has hacked into my soul and whatever I have planned, my soul will be open for him to read. No secrets. Therefore, the best plan of action is to have no plan and make him work for it. That's all I got.

Leah Silverwhisp

"Are you really going to make me work for it", a playful voice sounds in the back of mind.

"Yes," I answer him as I look down at my collection of papers that have built over the past week now sprawled out of my bed as if I were researching some ancient secret. *"I told you, Shev, you'd better get ready to run because I am not going to sit still and let you catch me."*

He chuckles and our brief conversation ends for now, but this is why I can't plan anything. I pick up one of the love poems I have written about a phantom wolf haunting his mate and then glance down at another poem about remaining grounded with the urge to fly. Maybe, I should finish the novel and get it published. I glance over at my laptop again; right now, I have three chapters each for my duet between me and my imagination of what he is up to since I don't have the same soul connection hack as him.

Leah Silverwhisp

"I dare you to write the whole book before I get there," Shev says, popping into my head again.

"Which is when exactly," I ask as I move off my bed and into my desk chair as I flip the screen of my laptop on. *"I could write this whole thing and get it published before you get here."*

"Maybe I want to read it first before you publish it," he teases.

"Nice try, wolf boy. If you really want to read it before I publish it, then I guess I could make an exception, but it is going to cost you the game," I tease as I pull up the document and start writing.

A growl sounds in the back of my mind causing me to giggle out loud. *"Haili, if I was there right now, I would bite you into submission starting with your lips and working my way down your body as I bite your neck, breasts, nipples, belly, and then your clit."*

I feel all the blood rush to my face as my hands stop moving on the keyboard. Don't

Leah Silverwhisp

think about it. Don't imagine it. Too late.
The imagery of him pinning me down on the
bed as his mouth moves from my lips to him
biting me all over, turning me on just
enough to tease me before a low chuckle
interrupts my thoughts bringing me back to
being alone in my room with him in my
head. All my thoughts have gone straight
into the gutter; if I think anything right now,
he will use it against me later. I just know it.
I have to distract myself with something,
anything. A knock sounds on my bedroom
door. I spin around in my chair to see who it
is, but the door remains closed.

"Haili, we are heading out to the grocery
shop for tomorrow. I need you to be out here
with Scooby in case he needs to go out,"
Mom says from the other side of my
bedroom door.

Oh shoot, tomorrow is the weekend.
Distraction acquired. "I'll be out in a few,
I'm just looking over homework for what I
have to do this week."

"Alright," she says before leaving with
Dad.

Leah Silverwhisp

Rooted Wings & Phantom Wolf

"I'll see you soon, darling," Shev teases before our soul conversation ends.

My face flushes slightly as I close my laptop shut and start getting ready for the day, which meant throwing on my sweatshirt and some pants. I grab my leaf green hoodie and a random pair of jeans that were lying about in an unfolded pile of laundry. I pull them on and slip out of the room to be greeted by a happy Scooby. I pat his head and walk into the living room. Tomorrow, I have to work at my part-time job that I longer want to be at and then when I get home from work, I will have to switch on to family mode because my sister will be over with her gang. Today is another story. Today I am home and have nothing better to do since I caught up on my schoolwork for the week. I knocked out the discussion posts fast and spilled all my thoughts onto my research paper. Now, all I have to do is take it easy and go over my paper cleaning it up to make it presentable as my first draft. However, that is next week's problem.

Today, I plan on writing my book and maybe reading a little bit. Though, right

Leah Silverwhisp

now, I look down at Scooby who has picked up a toy with his little tail wagging happily. I grab the roped legs of what I assume is either an octopus or a poorly made spider as we start to play tug of war. I hold my own as Scooby tries to free his toy from my grasp, pulling hard and harder until I let go letting him win. *Though Scooby is the only exception.* I smirk to myself and grab the toy away as we go for round two. I don't plan on losing anytime soon. I free the toy from Scooby's grasp and toss it down the hallway with him bounding after it. Shev may have the upper hand for now, but I don't just read tarot cards for divination practice. My true gift has always been enchanting items made from passion, and if I made them, the enchantments would be stronger. *Of course, I could create something now for later or—* A panting Scooby comes back with his toy and drops it at my feet interrupting my reverie. I toss the toy again and Scooby chases it. *Or—* I continue my thoughts *—I could use the archives.* I doubt Shev knows of them; I don't think about the archives as often as I should. I originally made a bunch of enchanting oils that have been steeping in

Leah Silverwhisp

my dresser drawer for years inside of a black and red lunchbox. I labeled each one for its purpose of enchanting. I have never used them, just let them steep in the darkness and hoped I would never need to use them. They were my insurance plan. In case my mundane life came crashing down in fire and smoke.

I don't think I will need the archives with Shev, I'll probably whip something out on the fly. The second I thought this, the image of Shev pinning my hands above my head as he straddles my body and ties my hands together flashes across my mind as Scooby licks my hand. I snap out of my thoughts and pat Scooby's head. "Oh, Scooby. I need Mom and Dad to hurry back home so I can escape back to my room and do some adult stuff."

A faint echo of Shev's words echoes in my head, *bite you into submission.* Would that happen after he traps me against his body and renders my hands useless? I glance down at my hands, now shiny from Scooby's love of licking my hands. I shuffle over into the kitchen as Scooby looks at me

Leah Silverwhisp

with concern. "I'm fine, Scooby, I just need something to eat or drink, and I will be good as new."

I open the fridge and spot the can of whipped cream. "I won't tell if you don't tell," I say, grabbing the whipped cream and bananas from the fridge. Then head over to the cabinet and take out two bowls. I split the banana in half and cut it into small pieces for each bowl before spraying the whipped cream. I put a spoon in mine and place Scooby's bowl down. I scoop up a piece of banana and whipped cream into my spoon as Scooby goes to town on his bowl. I giggle and put the spoon in my mouth as I do a little happy dance enjoying the flavors. I take another bite as I try to think about what to do today. I want to write, right?

I should go back to my room and write the book, otherwise I will never hear the end of it. Another spoonful of banana and whipped cream followed by another happy dance, and I find myself thinking about doing this in the house across the street waiting for Shev to come home. I freeze and look down at Scooby who was now all geared up for

51

Leah Silverwhisp

zoomies. I clean up his bowl and put it directly in the dishwasher. I quickly finish my bowl and glance over at Scooby. "I should probably walk you."

I grab the leash and use the sound of the clip to get Scooby to settle down enough for me to clip the leash onto his harness. "Good boy," I say, mushing his face. "Come on, let's go for a walk."

I unlock the front door and step outside of the house as Scooby hops out of the doorway. The front door closes as I pull the handle behind us, and I catch sight of the house being worked on. I carefully take a step forward onto the road as Scooby pads alongside of me. I need to get a grip, all I have is a hunch that is the house Shev will be moving into. That doesn't guarantee anything and I'm already thinking about living there. *Give in.* No, no. I walk away from the house with Scooby at my side and go down the block where I see a forest green SUV parked with a group of people looking at the corner house. A man yawns and grins with a smirk as the younger man complains about the older man's taste in music. The

Leah Silverwhisp

older one seems about my age and the younger one probably in his late teens or early twenties. Hard to tell, my brother has that youthful look, and he never looks his age. They both seems to be from up north, I can hear it in the tones of their voices. All I can tell from where I stand is that the man who is about my age is wearing a black baggy T-shirt and jeans and his companion just a shade lighter as they discuss how hellish the trip down here was. The rest of their group are discussing what to have for lunch, probably something healthier than bananas and whipped cream. I turn about to go back towards the house and start walking away.

By the time I get back to the house, Scooby seems to have taken care of all his outdoor business and worked off the whipped cream. Though, I'm sure zoomies will still happen once Mom and Dad returned from their shop. I freeze as soon as I approach the front door. There at the door is a stuffed wolf wearing a talisman around its neck. Scooby pulls me towards the stuffed wolf and sniffs it eagerly with his tail

Leah Silverwhisp

wagging and barks at me to let me know it's safe to pick up. "Good boy," I say, patting his head as I crouch down and pick up to see a note that it was sitting on.

I'll see you soon, darling. Let the games begin.

My heart starts to pound as I pick up the note and head into the house. I close the door behind me carefully and head towards the dining room table and place the wolf with the note on the door. Then I turn towards the security tablet on the counter that shows the front door. I open the camera feed and scroll through the recordings. There was me taking Scooby out and there was me returning with Scooby, no sign of the stuffed animal being brought to the house. No sign of anyone but me and Scooby. I kneel and unhook Scooby from his harness. I take the stuffed wolf and note back to my room and place them on my desk.

Leah Silverwhisp

Shevaron: Game On

After a joyful ride down South from Vermont, Selene and I go to the house we have rented to unload everything until we are ready to move into our new homes. She and Owen will run the big pack house while I will be in the new house across from Haili's alone. I won't be alone for too long, since I am planning to eventually have Haili live with me. Moments later, Owen shows up with the rest of the pack and sticks his head out the window. "They really want to see the house. Can I take them, or should we wait?"

"We should probably check on the progress in person," I say, rubbing the back of my head. "Adrian, can you stay behind and help Selene bring in the boxes off the moving truck? I'll take you by to see the house tomorrow."

Adrain hops out of the car and stretches out his limbs. "I was getting restless anyway."

55

Leah Silverwhisp

"Thank you," I say, turning towards the SUV and locking eyes with Jack who scurries off into the back seat. I slide into the passenger seat. "Do we have time to make a stop first?" I ask Owen as Selene and Adrian start bringing the boxes into the rental home.

Owen's green eyes study me closely for a short moment. "Where do you want to go?" he asks me curiously.

"To the mall, I have something to do there before we visit our new home," I say, leaning back against the seat with an idea already building in my mind. Now that I am so close to Haili, I can't just keep teasing her through soul connections. Time to step up my game.

"Alright, I need to buy clothes for Jack anyway. He loses his shirts faster than anyone in the pack," Owen says and puts the closest mall into his GPS.

"The girls wanted mementos," Jack grumbles in the back of the car.

The others laugh and I do too. Oh, to be that young and not have that significant

Leah Silverwhisp

connection yet. Jack probably likes all the attention the girls give him and how they always leave with something of his. No wonder, Owen and Selene have him in their phones as the shirtless one. That's his signature, giving a girl the shirt off his back just for the chance to see her smile. I wonder what he would do when that soul connection finally happens, what would he give to the one who haunts him as Haili does me.

Owen pulls away from the rental home and heads towards the mall as he plays the torture device that he used on Jack for the ride to South Carolina. I enjoy the sweet cringe of love songs sung by Owen and Selene together. No matter how cheesy the song was, Owen and Selene all went in. I absolutely love it and ask for a copy. Owen laughs and tells me I would have to ask Selene for the copy. Jack and the others discuss what stores to visit. I already have a plan in mind for what I want to do, I just hope that the mall will provide me with what I need to succeed.

Upon arrival, I send Owen and the pack to buy Jack clothes and a couple of other things that they need, while I head towards a particular store. I walk over the big colorful sign that reads Build-A-Bear, though I am not here for a bear. A step forward and I find myself in a sea of little kids with their parents stressing over what stuffed animal body to choose from. I walk over the gray wolf and pick it up, the one that mostly represented my wolf form, and head over to the voice box section. I pick one to record my voice and head over to the matching as I bring the voice box close to my mouth, leaving a playful message on it before I surrender what I have chosen over to the stuffer. The stuffer hands me a red heart and instructs me to do the wish dance. I follow the instructions to a T as I make a silent wish.

I leave the store with fifty dollars less than what I went in with and look down at the box in my hands. Inside is a little stuffed wolf that I named after myself. Though, the birth certificate will stay with me for now. I might give it to Haili later or I might not. Next stop, I head to the bookstore and pick out a couple of books that I know Haili has

Leah Silverwhisp

been reading. A series, that I consider to be one book. Another stand-alone series. A couple of stand-alone books. Books that I plan to use in our little game. I text Owen that I am ready to leave and tell him to meet me by the SUV. I head back to the car, while Owen finishes up shopping with the pack.

When Owen shows up, Jack has several bags filled with clothes just for him and the others have only one bag each. I can't help but laugh as Jack unloads all his bags into the truck. "You laugh now, but that stuffed animal you are holding brings me so much joy as our fearless pack leader has gone mad and made a stuffed animal at Build-A-Bear."

I put the box along with my bags of books on the passenger seat before I look over at Jack, while everyone else loads up into the SUV waiting for something to happen. Jack shifts nervously as he tries to quickly get into the car, but I hold the keys and lock the SUV as I step closer to him. "Don't be so hasty, Jack," I say as I pocket Owen's keys and look at Jack with a calm yet deadly smile, causing Jack to freeze where he stood. "We are about to visit our new home

59

after all, which means we will be near Haili, and I need you to do your job because what I made at Build-A-Bear is for her."

Jack's expression changes from fear to understanding, probably recalling the little talk that we had when packing up the truck. I smile and unlock the SUV before walking back around to my side of the car and handing the keys back to Owen after I juggle the bags and place them down in the middle of my feet. Jack gets back in quietly, pulls out his tablet and starts hacking into the camera system. I relax in the seat as Owen plugs in a basic address that is close enough to where we will be living since the new home development area has not been added in yet.

We drive in silence since Jack is hacking from his spot in the car; it takes about 45 minutes to reach our destination. Owen parks the car outside of the pack's house. There are still a bunch of construction workers around the building, landscaping the plots of land. I turn to Jack who gives me the thumbs up. "Alright, we won't turn

Leah Silverwhisp

up on anyone's cameras. Are you ready for what you need to do?"

I take out the stuffed wolf from the box and put a talisman around its neck that I picked out especially for her before we left Vermont. I borrow one of Selene's note pads that she keeps stashed in her car for when she is working and write down a playful note. Then my phone dings, letting me know that Haili is leaving the house. Most likely to take Scooby out for his scheduled walk, which means I'll have to loop around the other way. I exit the car with the gift I planned for her and stealthily sneak down the block before hers and come up the other side. Haili is walking further away from her house, so I walk up to her front porch and place the note and stuffed wolf just out of camera sight. Thankfully, the workers are too busy to notice anything strange going on as I travel back the same way I came and spot her from afar as she is watching the pack talking about food and Jack's painful experience of being trapped in the car with not only Selene but Owen too. I make

Leah Silverwhisp

myself scarce before she starts walking back up to her house.

Finally, back at the SUV I quickly get in and turn on the app that hacks into her cameras. Haili's expression as Scooby pulls her up to the porch is priceless, her beautiful blue eyes and thin sculpted eyebrows don't express fear. Her expression is more mixed than anything else, at first her brows lift in shock and surprise, but her eyes and perfectly pink lips say she is more curious, excited even to have something disrupt her daily mundane life. I desperately wish I could have seen it in person, but it's too soon. Being this close is dangerous enough as it is right now. My presence alone is enough to change things for her. Thankfully, Owen instructed me on what the proper distance is—at least a block away from her or I could trigger her to shift into her wolf form, causing things to happen too soon and she is not ready for that. Not for our world, at least. Things have been calm lately, but that can change at any moment. Owen gets back into the SUV with the rest of the pack and looks over at me.

Leah Silverwhisp

"We are in luck. Haili seems to be the only supernatural in the area. However, there are a couple of magick folk in the area. I am unsure if they are aware of their magick potential or not, but they are not a coven that is for sure," Owen reports back to me as everyone else settles in.

Leah Silverwhisp

Haili:

Magical Map Shifter Part 1

After I help Mom and Dad put away the groceries, I return to my bedroom and look at the stuffed wolf that sat on my desk. I pick it up and examine it closely. I stare at its eyes, squish its insides until an unfamiliar yet familiar deep voice comes from its paw. "Hello, darling, I can't wait to see what you have in store for me because I have so much in store for you."

I quickly glance at my bedroom door making sure no one heard that and only hear the television playing the news about how the state of the country is going. My shoulders slump in relief as I glance back at the stuffed wolf in my hands; he was here. Shev somehow evaded the cameras and left me with a cute little message. I squeeze the paw and hear his deep voice again, picking up on his playful happy tones in his voice. Damnit, I feel the blood rush to my cheeks. The difference between hearing his voice in my head and physically hearing his voice

Leah Silverwhisp

coming from the stuffed wolf makes me realize that Shev may very well be my kryptonite. I carefully place the stuffed wolf back onto my desk and sit in my chair running my hands over my face. I love the sound of his voice, and I want to hear more of it.

   No, I can't make it easy. I pick up the talisman that was around the stuffed wolf's neck and study it closely, noticing that it has two enchantments on it. One for protection and the other for recovery of magick. I put the talisman on and tuck it underneath my shirt as I consider my next move. I freeze and run straight to the bathroom. Crap, did he see me looking like this? My hair is an absolute mess; I had thrown into a messy ponytail not caring to brush it because I was just taking Scooby out on a quick walk. However, it looked like I slept in my ponytail causing my thin brown hair to clump together revealing my scalp. I also went out without a bra in one of my big sweatshirts to hide my chest and pajama pants. I really need to rethink my lazy days

Leah Silverwhisp

off because this will not do. This is just too embarrassing.

I return to my desk and sit in my chair as I open my laptop back up. My screen lights up to the word document that I had opened. I glance at it then to the deck that sat next to the stuffed wolf and wonder if I should give it a quick shuffle to see how what I am about to do will affect me. I reach over and pick up the deck shuffling it in my hand and draw a card. I freeze at the sight of the card: Magical Shape Shifter. Excuse me. I flip through the guidebook, find the card's page and read it carefully. *To make you aware of the people who come into your life to impact your personal growth. Perhaps you may meet a soul mate whose presence invites you to be the best "you" that you can be.*

I reach for my phone and pause as I wonder if I should tell anyone what has been happening. It's not like I can contact or call anybody and tell them what has been happening to me these past couple of months. I put my phone down and plug it into the charger.

66

Leah Silverwhisp

I turn back to the document on my desk and unleash everything into my writing, compelled to spill every hidden thought – whimsical idea – and emotion down the pages. One page turns into five, and five pages turn into nineteen pages, and so many words later, I have chapters and characters running rampant on my keyboard as I can't stop. The screen starts to blur and gets out of focus, to which I hit the save option on the word document and glance at the clock in the corner of my screen. 3:00 a.m. I blink and rub my eyes to make sure I wasn't seeing things. 3:01 a.m. A yawn escapes my mouth as I stretch, thinking that I have to work later. Oh shoot, it's the weekend too. I have to socialize and not hide in my room like the book hermit that I am. Though this week's writing marathon has made one thing very clear to me. I've never felt better.

I'll admit I am having way too much fun writing, reading, and even teasing this year ever since Shev started making his move. I am trying to not let everything get away from me, I still have school, and I still have to go to work, which ugh I don't want to deal with the drama that goes on there. And maybe I let these responsibilities distract me from my purpose for too long. Maybe I can finally spread my wings safely and trust myself to soar up into the sky and not crash into the ground. Just maybe I can trust in myself and not be afraid of my own emotions.

   Soon after those thoughts crossed my mind, I fall asleep at my desk. When I wake up, I hear Scooby barking at my door for his early morning walk. I yawn sleepily as I look at the screen that showed several complete chapters and smirk proudly to myself. At this pace, I might get this published before Shev arrives. Though technically he was already here. He made that clear yesterday. I sit up in my chair and look over at the stuffed wolf that still sat on my desk. Very much real. Yup, no denying it now. I move out of my chair and scramble over to my bedroom door and open it as Scooby pounces on me. I hook him up to his harness, then take him outside to go to the bathroom as I yawn sleepily. I glance at the house in front of ours, noticing that they

Leah Silverwhisp

finally have windows put up. Damn, they work fast. I walk Scooby around the driveway especially since I have to get ready for work soon and I can't be late because Mom and Dad have plans to have people over later.

  I am in desperate need for a coffee, but a shower must come first. I look down at Scooby and sigh as he pulls me back towards the house after he was done. "I'll have Mom walk you again, bud. I need to shower and drink a few cups of coffee."

Leah Silverwhisp

Haili:

Magical Map Shifter Part 2

I take Scooby back inside the house, pass Mom the leash and leave the main area of the house to take a well needed shower. Hot water rains down on my skin as I step into the shower and pull the green shower curtain closed. My hands rub the hot water into my face. *Come on, Haili, wake up.* For a moment, my naked body does nothing but stand there as the hot water falls onto my skin. By the time I convince myself to grab the purple luffa that was falling apart and start scrubbing dragons' blood bodywash into my pale skin except for the one colorful spot on my left shoulder where I was tattooed, I know that I may run a little bit late if I don't pick up the damn pace.

In my attempts to start getting to work, I search for an outfit that matches the requirements of retail stores in the south. This retail store that sells a lot of shoes and country vibe fashion has a uniform code that

70

Leah Silverwhisp

consists of a pair of jeans and a simple blouse with sneakers that the store sells. No sweatshirts, no tank tops, and no T-shirts. However, western boots and hats were allowed to showcase the country style that has embraced the area, especially since a lot of rodeos and country concerts are always trending. Not for me. I have never been one to follow trends or embrace the country's southern fashion. For instance, today's outfit will consist of a sage waffle blouse that mimics a T-shirt style with a pair of jeans and a pair of light orange sneakers with black laces, which do not exist in any of our store's inventory. Don't get me wrong, the store has brands and similar models in colors that just don't scream Haili. Therefore, I ordered directly from the band and still fall in lines of shoes you can wear to work. Though at some point I do need to clean these since Scooby did drag me through the clay, while we were out for one of our walks. Thankfully, the orange hides it well.

For once, I am looking forward to going to work because I don't have to stress about getting ready for having company over. At work, I could focus on what I needed to get done and not be forced into awkward conversations in which my responses will not satisfy the vultures that wait with eager eyes.

Travel cup, check. Hot coffee, check. Caramel macchiato creamer, check.

On the way to work, I try to revive myself with the hot coffee in my Avengers' travel cup. The odds seem to be working against me as I sip my coffee—the hot delicious liquid only does enough to jolt my system into action, but my eye lids still feel heavy. I should probably go to bed early tonight. A yawn escapes my lungs as my dad eyes me from the driver's seat of the car.

"What time did you go to bed last night?" he asked me curiously.

My eyes focus on the road in front of us. "I never made it to my bed."

"Haili," my dad says with a 'what am I going to do with you' sigh.

Leah Silverwhisp

"Wha-at," I say exasperatedly. "Listen, falling asleep at one's desk is a rite of passage for any graduate student." Though I was writing my book since I have completed my graduate school homework.

"You need to take care of yourself too, Haili," he says as he turns left. "I need you to take care of yourself and be more disciplined in your choices."

"I know," I say, taking a big gulp of coffee. "I just didn't want to lose the momentum."

"Momentum can work against you," Dad points out. "You could run the marathon and build up the momentum to surpass your limits momentarily on the track, but you lose the ability to control your pace. Then when an obstacle appears on the track, avoidance isn't an option anymore. You are going to crash right into it."

"Life makes so much more sense now," I say, taking a sip of my coffee.

"Haili," Dad says more seriously. "I need you to take it easy and pace yourself."

73

Leah Silverwhisp

"Alright," I say with a soft smile as we arrive at my job. "I promise to pace myself and not pull all-nighters."

Before exiting the car, I hug him and tell him that I'll see him later when I get off shift. Then head into work. I push open the doors and enter the fabulous world of customer service, where customers push your limits, and your coworkers test your tolerance levels. I scan the store to see who I'll be working with today and notice that everyone has kind of scattered to different parts of the store. *Oh, it's going to be one of those days.* Often, I find myself alone in the front of store, while my lovely coworkers obscure to the back of the store to either hide in the bathroom to be on their phones, have conversations in the breakroom, or choose to break down boxes in order to avoid customers. I'm not sure if it's trust or just out of convenience for them. I stopped caring a long time ago; almost everyone responds to my summons when I need to return – exchange – layaway – and special order an item from another store location.

Leah Silverwhisp

First things first, I walk over to the register and clock myself so I would be on time for my shift and then step out of the register area to go straighten up my department. A yawn escapes my mouth as I start laser lining the shoes until someone walks into my aisle and starts talking to me.

"Hey, Haili," a familiar female voice says as I look up to my least favorite coworker. "I didn't realize you came in, how was your day off yesterday?"

Enry, the country princess and one of the managers on duty today. "Hey, Enry, my day off was productive. I had to get ready for midterm grades. A lot of due dates are coming up."

"Jeez, do you ever take a break?" she asks, doing none of the work that needs to be done. Her department has been torn up pretty good with jeans spilling out of the shelves and shirts halfway falling off their hangers.

"I take breaks," I retort. For food and sometimes sleep. Maybe I am a little bit distracted from other things happening in

75

Leah Silverwhisp

my life right now, but I do take breaks. The question is, do I rest during those breaks? Nope, my attempts to sleep are often interrupted by my soul and I can't sleep until I can get this itch out of my system. My usual attempts of burning it off with some form of physical activity in bed whether it's teasing my clit until I can't take it or just listening to an audiobook that I love. Both seem to help my mind shut off a lot faster, but there are some things that can't be helped. For instance, my writing marathon, I spill everything out until my mind has nothing left to give. Then I try to get comfy in my bed as I wrap my sage green comforter around my naked body, because I absolutely despise sleeping with clothes on. Sleep doesn't come. Instead, the pulsating impulses of creative thoughts and inspiration demand my attention, and I am forced to make a choice. Either I leave my place of comfort and sit at my desk to write more, or I bring my laptop to my bed and write there.

"Right," she says with a bit of sarcasm in her voice.

Leah Silverwhisp

I chat with Enry for a little bit more while I work, and she does nothing. The rest of my shift consists of falling into the busy workflow and almost falling asleep on my break. When it's time to clock out for my shift, I'm relieved that it's over. However, it's too early to celebrate.

Shevaron:

The Rental House

I can't help but smirk when I soul connect with Haili. Her social battery has drained significantly in the course of two hours. Not only did she experience a huge lunch rush of customers coming into the shop with their families but her tolerance for Enry's laziness is beginning to wane thin. Every eyeroll Haili makes, I have to suppress my amusement and hold back in a laugh. Though, I hate to say it, Haili has no poker face. Her big beautiful blue eyes and thin sculpted eyebrows are so expressive that they betray her. Unfortunately for Haili, her eyerolls were a dead giveaway to how she truly feels about Enry.

My fingers drum on the makeshift table that Owen has set up for us inside the rental house. Haili's shift is finally ending and with another soft push, our soul connection intensifies causing both of our souls to ignite. *"Did you like my gift?"*

Leah Silverwhisp

Her face suddenly gets hot as she recalls the stuffed wolf with the recording of my voice. *"What gift?"*

Oh, she's trying to hide it from me. Come on, Haili, you know better than that. *"Oh, you know,"* I growl playfully.

"Are you talking about the tease you left me with," she says, her face blushing hard, while she tries to hide it from her mom who has picked her up from work. *"I loved it, and I have been brainstorming ideas to how I should tease you in return."*

A warm smile spreads across my face. *"I can't wait to see what you will do, darling."*

"Oh, the game is just getting started, love," she teases.

Then our conversation is over as she gets home safely to only be met with the rest of her family. I couldn't distract Haili anymore for the day. Besides the stuffed wolf will do that all on its own. Meanwhile, Selene who is sitting across from me has not once looked up from her MacBook pro as she moves her mouse while editing her videos.

Leah Silverwhisp

Her focus amazes me sometimes; I had this whole soul connection conversation in front of her and she was just working away like nothing else was happening, not even asking me about why I had grown so quiet or why I was making a face.

Selene keeps working without issue until Owen comes into the dining room. "How did your soul conversation go with Haili?"

My eyes land on Selene and not Owen as I catch a slight smirk on her face as she now pretended to work. Without looking away from Selene, I say, "It went great, Haili is planning her revenge on me for the gift I left her."

Selene now grins. "You know, I haven't seen the house yet. Maybe I should visit and give Haili some tips while I'm there."

"Selene," I say, now locking my eyes on hers. "No one is allowed to approach Haili, unless something happens."

"Aye, aye, Captain," Selene salutes me. "I shall not approach your mate unless something happens."

Leah Silverwhisp

"Thank you. How's your newest project coming along?" I ask, genuinely curious about it.

"Almost finished." She beams excitedly. "This month's theme of course has to be food, and I have been researching all different kinds of dishes to try here in the south. I'm most excited about trying fried pickles."

Finally, I look over at Owen who is holding a bag of groceries. "And you recruited the mad food scientist to this project?"

"Yup," she says as she continues to edit her video on her laptop. "He volunteered as tribute to go along with me on this project."

Jack comes crashing into the room snatching the bag of groceries out of Owen's hands, stumbling as he tries to regain his balance and opens the bag to find two bottles of hot sauce made from two of the hottest peppers in the world, the reaper and the ghost pepper. His eyes meet Owen's mad grin. "I'm ordering takeout," he says resolutely as he places the bags down on the

81

Leah Silverwhisp

table carefully before pulling out his phone to call in a pizza. I watch Jack leave the room more gracefully than he entered.

Selene snickers to herself as she picks up one of the bottles. "You were supposed to hide this a lot better, Owen, now I have to rethink my plan."

Owen smirks. "That was the red herring." He takes out a smaller bag from his pocket. "I kept the real trick hidden for later."

Now, it's my turn to roll my eyes. "Must you two always mess with Jack?"

Just then Adrian walks in with a collected stack of job applications and copies of his resume. Selene and Owen share a look before turning their attention to Adrian. "Job applications?" one of them asks.

"Yeah," he says as he places his stack into four different piles. "Not only for me, though. I also grabbed applications and made resumes for Sam, Tyler and Cleo as well."

I pick up the stacks of paper and combine them together. "I want the four of you to really think about what you want to do. Work, school, whatever you want to do. You have until the day we move to decide. Until then explore every avenue."

After advising Adrian, I leave the dining room and head into my makeshift office of pack affairs where I pick up a manila folder from my desk. *Alright, enough fooling around.* I open the folder and sit on top of my desk. Nothing has been reported. No signs of supernatural activity. No one is disrupting the peace or threatening to expose us, yet an unsettling feeling lingers in the back of my mind. Something about this feels off to me. Things are too quiet, too clean. The file in my hands is lacking something, a missing piece of this haunting puzzle.

Jack slides into the room with a giant slice of pizza hanging down from his mouth and offers me a slice of his massive pizza box. I shake my head and say, "Can you dig around and see what's going on?"

He eyes the file in my hand as he tears the slice away from his mouth and swallows. "Sure thing," he says before taking another

Leah Silverwhisp

bite of his slice. "I'll do some digging and see what's up."

Haili: Sacred Pool

The entire drive home is torture as Mom tries to question me about why I am smiling so much. My cheeks start to hurt as I try to relieve the pain by biting the inside of my cheeks trying to stop myself from smiling. By the time we arrive home, my cheeks feel sore, and Mom has only grown more suspicious. I glance over at the house across the street and feel that all too familiar tug as the construction workers continue to build up the house. To walk through that doorway, to be welcomed home. I turn back towards my mom and follow her inside as I mentally note revisiting the feeling later.

Inside, I am met with hugs as my niece and nephew run up to hug me tightly. "Aunty!"

I scoop them up into big hugs. "Oh my goodness, you guys are getting so big!"

My sister walks over and hugs me too, "You're late."

"I had to work," I say, hugging her back as the kids return to playing with Scooby.

85

Leah Silverwhisp

"You have a degree, why aren't you using it? Or are you just going to stay in school for the rest of your life and not take the next step," she says in a caring but stinging way.

"Umm ouch," I say as I put my stuff down and turn to her. "You don't need to worry about that. That is my job, not yours. Yes, I have a degree, and I could be doing something with it. However, what I do with it is my choice. I earned that degree myself and what I want to do with it involves me continuing my education and getting my Masters."

"I just," she starts to say, but I look at her dead on.

"You just want me to succeed and not be a burden to our parents because I still live at home with them." I lean up against the hallway. "Listen to me, okay. I love you and I understand where you are coming from all too well. I really do, but I am thirty-one years old, and I know what I am doing. I put in the work and get things done at my own pace and I need you to understand that. I'm

86

Leah Silverwhisp

not perfect, but I get it done. Make it work, remember."

My sister stares at me blankly, I don't think she has seen me stand my ground before like this. I'm not sure what has gotten into me, but I look over to see the kids still distracted by Scooby and our parents with my brother-in-law watching us cautiously as if we were about to brawl. I push off the wall and smile at her. "Give me some credit, I'm your sister and you were the one who encouraged me to fly."

If one could manifest wings, I'd imagine I just did as I felt a pair of fiery wings burn brightly as they grew out of my back. I stride into the kitchen, grab a coke from the fridge and crack the can open causing it to hiss before I take a sip. Everyone seems to be watching me carefully. I place the can down on the counter and look over at the kids who aren't paying us attention as Scooby continues to entertain them. My attention back on everyone else, deciding what I am going to say next.

Leah Silverwhisp

"So," I say simply as I watch my sister finally recover and walk into the kitchen. "How is everyone else doing today, what's new?"

"Haili, can we talk about what just happened?" my sister asks, looking at me pleadingly.

"Nope." I shake my head as I take another sip of my coke. *You don't want me to, trust me. Let me sweep it under the rug for another day, please.* "You are here visiting with the kids, and I just came home from work. I would love some stress-free family time."

She shakes her head, and I sigh deeply before downing my can of coke quickly. I grab her cold hands and drag her out the front and away from the kids. I turn towards her and let go of her hand. Where do I even begin with her? "You really want to do this right now?"

"Yes," she says, looking at me trying to figure out. "What has gotten into you, Haili?"

Leah Silverwhisp

Good question, what has gotten into me? I think about the past couple of months. The bullshit at work has gotten worse between the favoritism and princess syndrome that has caused the positivity of the job to drop significantly. Then there was graduate school, I have to hold myself accountable for turning everything in on time and make sure I make it to the live lectures that stream to my laptop. All those due dates and time schedules, I have to say no to a lot of things and make sure I am doing my part. I know I make it sound easy, but it's not. There were times when I had to be selfish, 'Sorry, I can't come into work. I have a research paper to write' – 'Sorry, I can't hang out with you, I have class tonight' – 'Sorry, school is my number one priority.' Oh, and let's not forget that I have been on this reading spicy books kick, where I now have a building collection growing in my closet. Mom and Dad don't know how fast it's growing, but the collection almost extends across the entire top of my dresser. And that doesn't include the audiobooks on my phone and the books I have on pre-order. Yeah, I may be a little bit of a book dragon and a book worm.

Leah Silverwhisp

"Haili," my sister says, getting impatient as my thoughts ramble on and on.

Now, I haven't told anyone about Shev or that his soul connection to me started a couple of years ago and nothing has come from it except for periods of time where our souls touch. At first, I started leaving messages for him in a small glass jar from the dollar store and put inside of a small stump in the wood behind our house. I hoped he would find it and write back to me. Or show up randomly with the jar in his hands, but all that did was leave me disappointed. After a while, things started to quiet down, until he made a playlist in my head and our souls started touching. Want to talk about a distraction? This happened a lot while I was working. Oh, then when I was alone at the mall to enjoy my 'single' dates where I would treat myself to some books and a good meal, I would feel the faintness of a hand interlocked with mine. Then things quieted down again for a while and life got busy. Now. Now, he was playing dirty. Not only did we soul connect and have full on conservations with each other, but now there

Leah Silverwhisp

was a stuffed wolf in my room with his recorded voice. Oh boy, all of this made me want to write and give myself in to the writing deities completely to convey how much I loved this man that I haven't even met yet. Which brings me back to the question at hand, what has gotten into me? Absolutely nothing.

"Nothing," I finally answer. "My filter may be broken, though."

My sister folds her arms and gives me the 'really' look with the raised eyebrow. "Haili."

"I'm serious, I have been focusing on myself lately. You know, cleaning up bad habits and picking up good ones. I started to get back to the roots that are me and whether you like it or not, I'm good with my life right now. Not only am I succeeding in school, but I also plan on leaving my toxic retail job so I can focus on getting to graduation. If that isn't enough proof for you, I am enjoying reading and writing again," I explain, feeling my soul burn so brightly as Shev connects into me as if to show his support. "Nothing has gotten into me."

"Yet, " Shev teases.

Oh shush, you. "I just gotten back to the roots of who I am and ignited the fire inside of me that has caused my filter to break."

"Not the only thing that will break, " Shev says as I glance at the security camera for a brief moment.

I'm trying to have a serious conversation here, Shevaron. "I understand that you feel like you need to watch out for me, advise me, and micro analyze everything I do. I know you do it out of love and that's why I tolerate it, but it does get on my nerves, and I let it get to me. You know, I stopped reading because of you. You called it an escape and said what I was doing was unhealthy. It turned me off to reading. For years, my 'to be read' pile has been building up over time because I let you get to me. I'll admit, I wasn't strong enough then to say fuck it and continue to read anyway."

Leah Silverwhisp

"And now," she asks, sadly looking hurt with tears in her eyes.

"Now," I say, hugging her close to me. "We hug and I tell you that my taste in books has changed and I'm so much stronger that no one or nothing can get into me."

"Unless it's me," Shev adds before the soul connection fades out.

The rest of the night is normal after my sister and I rejoin the family for dinner. Later, I excuse myself to turn in for the night. Once back in my room, I close the door behind me and stride back over to my desk where the stuffed wolf sat taunting me. *Alright, time to make a move.* I spin around and walk straight over to my closet and open the door before squatting down to open the dresser drawer that reveals an anime collectable lunch box. I open it up and hold up a small bottle that's labeled 'Light'. *Not sure, if this will work,* I think as I prep open the bottle and drip it onto the palm of my left hand. My eyes close as I visualize a ball of light in the palm of my left hand being

93

Leah Silverwhisp

empowered by the potent oil of light enchanting oil. I open my eyes and the ball of light sits in my hand. I walk over to the stuffed wolf and carefully place the ball of light inside of the stuffed wolf without damaging it. I hold my hand on the stomach of the stuffed wolf for about five seconds as the enchantment takes hold.

"That should hold," I say as I check to see if any enchantment oil remained. None remained, which was good. It meant I could finally sleep with peace of mind. I flop down into my bed with the stuffed wolf and press its paw to hear Shev's voice again before falling asleep.

Leah Silverwhisp

Shevaron: Round One

A couple of months have passed since then, and Haili is finally leaving her toxic retail job. I'll miss teasing her while she works. I sit at my desk as I watch her work on her last day from the desk, while I work on documents for an AI to use. On the glamorous side of my job, I scroll through and edit various documents before the AI can even touch them. I fix small grammatical errors, make sure keywords that the AI would recognize are in there and make sure that the document has enough clarity for the AI to understand. Boring, I know but hey someone has to do it.

Jack walks into my office holding a big cup of coffee in his hands. "I know why everyone is being so quiet and you are not going to like it," he says, yawning, and sits his coffee cup down on my desk before sitting down in one of the open chairs. Jack looks stressed, more than usual. Whatever he has uncovered must be bad if he had to go that far into the abyss to find out why the

Leah Silverwhisp

whole supernatural community here is being quiet.

"What did you find?" I ask as I watch Haili interact with her customers while she works.

He pulls out a thumb drive from his pocket and places it on the table. "They're waiting for the *shift in the veil to happen*." Jack leans back in his chair as he pauses. "In their encrypted notes and whispers to each other, they speak about plans for a kidnapping and uprising in the country, in order to fix what is broken beyond repair."

"Ugh, we are dealing with revolutionaries," I groan. They are a pain to handle because it usually meant that I have to social my way through hoops of supernatural customs. Just stop the revolution before it happens. "Is that all?"

Jack grows quiet; I look up from my laptop and see his grim expression. "The *shift in the veil* refers to a person, not a particular event, Shev."

I freeze and stare at the screen on my laptop that has security footage of Haili

Leah Silverwhisp

working at her job; she's laser lining the boxes again. My hand moves for the flash drive and I stick it onto the computer. A couple of clicks later, I see the abyss of Jack's research. Chat logs, encrypted files detailing specific dates and times. Addresses lined up and highlighted. A couple of names listed in their notes. A low growl escapes my throat as my blood boils with anger. Jack was right. I don't like it. In fact, I want to rip out their throats or gauge out their eyes, probably both. More than anything, though, I want to run to Haili and keep her safe in my arms away from it all.

Fuck, the house isn't ready for her yet. It isn't move-in ready yet, and I haven't even made a proper move yet other than a stuffed wolf at her doorstep. I know she made a move, but I absolutely have no idea what she has done just yet. However, one thing is clear. I need to make a move soon and stick to the plan.

"Hack into her phone and laptop," I tell Jack and close out of the file before handing him the flash drive back. "Also, let the others know I am heading out."

Leah Silverwhisp

"At least tell me where you are going," Jack asks, pocketing the flash drive back into his left pocket. One look at Jack and he puts his hands up in surrender. "Got it, ask questions later. I'll get the job done, boss."

Without another word, I leave the rental home and end up back in the new home development where Haili lives. *Our* house is almost ready; it has no floors or appliances yet. I walk through the building knowing she won't be home just yet. I see her mom outside watering the plants. She looks over at me and smiles, waving her hand in a friendly gesture. I give a friendly wave back and walk over to her casually. "Hello, I was just checking in on the progress of the house, while I had some free time. I'm Shevaron, but I mostly go by Shev."

"Oh, a new neighbor," she says excitedly. "My name is Rita, I moved into the community with my husband and daughter last fall. Your home should be ready soon, they are pretty quick."

"Nice to meet you, Rita, and that is amazing news," I say, smiling and chatting

98

Leah Silverwhisp

with her. "Right now, I'm renting a home with a couple of friends who also bought a home in the community. We escaped the business of the north and found our way to the south."

"Oh, that's so sweet. Why didn't you guys get a house together, if you don't mind me asking?"

Because I want Haili to have her own space as she adjusts to her new lifestyle after she shifts for the first time. "I wanted my own personal library and office because I work from home as a data annotator."

"If you could only see my daughter's room, she is slowly but surely turning her room into a book nook," she says, smiling.

"Your daughter sounds like an awesome person. I would love to meet her one day," I say before checking my phone to see a text message from Owen. "Unfortunately, I have to go. I've been summoned by my friends to help with grocery shopping. It was so nice meeting you, Rita."

Leah Silverwhisp

I head back to Selene's SUV and drive back to the rental home where I find the others watching me pull up from the front steps. Selene moves first in her powder blue pajamas and taps on the window. I roll down the window. "Hi."

"Don't you hi me, Shevaron, where on earth did you go with my car?"

"I just visited the house," I say casually as I turn off the engine.

"And…" She waits for me to continue.

"And I made my next move in the game I have going on with Haili," I say with a wolfish grin forming on my lips as I imagine her shocked expression when her mother mentions my name in conversation. This is going to drive her nuts, and I can't wait to see what she will do to retaliate.

Leah Silverwhisp

Haili: Golden Palace

After I leave work for the last time, Mom picks me up and starts telling me about her day. She tells me about her early morning walk with Scooby and how she got a lot done around the house. Laundry, dishes, prepping for dinner and watering the plants. The usual daily activities, including walking down to the mailbox and back.

"Sounds like a productive day," I say with a smile as I lean back. It feels so weird that I won't be returning to work. At least not in the same way, maybe as a customer. I have a feeling that I should stay away from the dumpster fire that was about to blow up, though.

"Oh, and I met a new neighbor today, his name is Shevaron and he works as a data annotator," Mom says excitedly. "His house will be the one that is right across from ours. I get a good vibe about him and kind of reminds me of that marvel hero you like, Thor? The one that is played by Chris Hemsworth."

Leah Silverwhisp

I – uh – um – did I – just hear that right. "Did I just hear you right, that you met our new neighbor who could possibly be the Norse god of lightning?"

"His name is Shevaron, but he goes by Shev," Mom says, laughing at my question.

Thank goodness her eyes were on the road or else she would see all my blood rushing to my face. He got me so good this time. How am I supposed to match that? He has always been in control, hiding in the shadows as I was at his mercy. "That is a cool name."

"I dare you to say it," he teases in my head.

"Right, I love meeting people with cool names." Mom beams happily as I flush deeper and look out the window trying to hide my face.

"Shevaron, kind of sounds like it's out of a fantasy book," I say, trying to relax my smile as my cheeks start to hurt.

"I can't wait to hear you say it in person," he teases. *"And moan it in our bed."*

Leah Silverwhisp

Evil, I think to myself. My mind takes the damn bait and lands straight in the gutter. I imagine him towering over me on the big bed with no room for me to escape as he rails me hard. Each thrust of his hips causes sounds that I have never made before escape my throat as I say his name.

Get your mind out of the gutter, Haili, I scold myself. You are talking to your mother, and you will not fall for his horny trap. In climbing myself out of the dirty gutter of my mind, I bite the inside of my cheek and snap back into reality. Oh look, we are almost home.

"Sorry, Mom, I completely spaced out. I was thinking about an idea for a book," I say as she eyes me suspiciously for a second but then it's gone.

"That mind of yours, I swear. How many worlds live inside your head?"

If only she knew that the only thing that truly lived in my head was one very horny and evil wolf whom she met in person today. "I'm honestly not sure, I think maybe it's the

Leah Silverwhisp

same world and I just keep transforming it in order to answer different questions."

"I think you're the horny one, imagining me railing you on a king size bed," he teases as Mom pulls up into the driveway.

Mom parks the car in the garage and soon enough we are back in the house. Scooby comes pounding towards me with joy. "Hey boy!"

I smush his bearded face in my hands as he licks me happily. I give him a treat from my bag and head over to my bedroom and close the door behind me. I am finally free from my job, but from school no. I still have to finish the semester and get ready for the next one, my last one. Also, I still have to publish the book. I have about finished it and yet the perfectionist inside of me wanted to beat it.

I look at the stuffed wolf that I have now moved to my bed as I sleep with it every night. He met my mom. Talked to her. Shev introduced himself to her knowing very well that I was at work. Well played, wolf boy. Well played. It's my turn for real this time as Shev has started becoming bolder in his

104

movements. I turn to my laptop that lays closed on my desk.

This is no time to be stumped; the stuffed wolf I enchanted was more for me and not for retaliation. I just didn't want the voice recorder to die and so it gets recharged every time I hug the stuffed wolf. I could send the draft to my publisher and go forward with my book. However, I am not satisfied with it yet. No, I have to really retaliate this time and got nothing because he has the advantage. I let a growl of frustration escape my throat as I plop down on my bed, and I really need to do something about this horniness.

My eyes catch sight of one of my dragon pendants hanging from the top shelf of my bookcase. It glistens as the light from the ceiling hits the stone in the center. An idea starts to formulate in my mind as I sit up from my bed and go back to the archives, but this time I pull out the sacred wood oil. This one is my favorite to use when it is enchanting because it smells amazing and it's super strong. It's a combination of nine wood sacred to Druidry: small pieces of

Leah Silverwhisp

applewood, ash, birch, cedar, fir, hawthorn, oak, rowan or sandalwood, and willow mixed together.

I make my way over to the bookcase and lift the jade dragon statue that holds my dragon pendant in place. The pendant falls into my hand as I place the statue back down. If he has eyes on me, I might as well return the favor. The sacred oil drips onto the stone as I call the dragon out of the pendant. A small smile forms on my lips.

"Hello, Penn Craft," I say to the small teal scaled dragon with wings in the palm of my hand. "You are going to be my eyes."

Leah Silverwhisp

Shevaron: Round 2

Jack in his box fortress of electronics is hacking away into Haili's electronics, while I observe patiently from the doorway of his bedroom. A couple of moments pass, and I wonder how long he'll make me stand here. I lean up against the doorframe watching him as he clicks away at the computer.

"And we are in," Jack exclaims and tosses me back my phone. "You now have access to her laptop and cell phone."

I catch my phone. "Thank you." I immediately tap into the app and pull up Haili's phone.

On the screen, I get a view of Haili in her bedroom sitting on her desk with a little dragon perched on her shoulder. The little dragon puffs and delights as she scratches underneath its chin. It glances at her phone and pounces on it acting playful. Yet, I turn up the volume waiting to hear *her* voice.

"Penn Craft, you silly dragon. It isn't time yet, silly," her sweet voice comes over the phone.

107

Aww she named it. What will she have you do, little Penn Craft? I look over at Jack who has put on his headphones and started working on his computer again. I slide out of the room and head back to my own bedroom.

"Penn, I need him to show up, so you can put eyes on him," she tells the little dragon as it puffs in response to her. "He needs to make a move first, that way I can have you track him."

I hum with delight as I swipe off the app and put my phone away. Haili, Haili, Haili. I'm going to have so much fun with this, you don't even know.

The next day, Selene and Owen come with me to the bookshop. There, I pick up a few items. I grab an oracle deck, along with a journal with a wolf on it and a weighted pen. Selene picks out a few books herself. Owen a couple of cooking books that he could experiment with, which he didn't need. They only came along with me while Jack and the others were making their final decisions about what they would do in the fall.

Though, Jack was only assisting them in their research before they made their choice.

Selene bounces over to Owen with a beaming smile. "This month's book-topic is going to be a true delight."

"What are you guys in the mood for?" he asks. "German, Italian or Asian," Owen asks, holding up two regular cookbooks and one anime cookbook.

"Let's do Asian, the kids will love it," I say with a smile as we get in line to check out. "Also, there's a meeting tonight. Don't be late."

Their faces grow serious as I say the last part. A pack meeting. I haven't called one since I decided to move to South Carolina. Fall is right around the corner, and I can't waste any more time. Jack has been hard at work trying to keep tabs on the revolutionaries. They were still quiet, but the closer we get to Haili's birthday, the more I want to reveal myself to her. To confirm her sanity and embrace her in my arms. Protect her from all who threaten her, though I very well know she can handle herself. After all,

Leah Silverwhisp

she just called on a dragon to gain an upper hand on me. I'm sure she can do a lot more, especially when her power will be at its highest.

Yet, that will also mean putting her through so much pain as her body destroys itself to make another. However, I can't keep putting it off. Especially, if they decide to go after *her*. I can't let that happen.

Once back at the house, I call the meeting as I send Selene and Owen to round up the pack and meet in the living room. There, I stand in front of the fireplace with my hands behind my back as the rest of the pack file into the room and take their seats on the couch. Owen is the only one to remain standing as he leans up against the doorway, nodding to me.

"Jack has uncovered a secret group of revolutionaries who are lying in wait to make a move when the veil starts to thin. We believe their target involves someone who will be shifting for the first time when this is to happen. Each of you will shadow a name on this list and if you notice anything

Leah Silverwhisp

suspicious, let me know immediately. I will be contacting our allies in Vermont to lend a hand," I instruct, carefully keeping a firm grip on my hands. "If this were any normal supernatural disturbance, I would be running point, but I need Owen to take point and handle the surveillance with Jack."

Selene raises her hand. "What is your plan?"

My grip gets tighter as I think about how to answer her. "I am going to continue the plan and have Haili shift before her birthday, which means I can't be around to run point."

Owen looks over at me. "Her name landed on the list, didn't it?"

"It did," I say, feeling that same crushing feeling in my chest. I should be by her side right now, reading books to her as I wait for this storm to pass. I want her nowhere near this world, that is why I stayed away from her. Yet, time has other plans. Her body is getting ready to shift, and time has been counting down for years. Haili got to live a normal life, she got to live a pretty mundane life with her friends and family.

Leah Silverwhisp

But now, Haili is about to meet the supernatural world with everything that comes along with it, including the dangers. I have to make my next move and speed things along, even though the damn house isn't ready yet.

"Owen, Jack has all the information you need. Assign everyone to their respected charges to shadow. I'm heading out and borrowing Selene's SUV," I say, picking up the bag from the bookstore and grabbing the keys off the hook.

Once I am in the SUV, I start it up and drive straight to the community and pull up by the mailbox setup. I step out of the car and pick her number box open, then place my gifts inside minus the entire deck of oracle cards. I only used one oracle card from the deck that I hid within the journal's pages. I look up to see her walking down the hill with Scooby and Penn Craft chilling on top of her head, invisible to the human eye.

I let Penn see me before closing the mailbox up and getting back into the SUV. I slowly pull out and start driving away as

Leah Silverwhisp

Penn leaps off her head to start following me. Penn lands on top of the SUV as I exit back onto the road and head back to the rental.

Haili: Scots Pine

Penn Craft is on the move towards the mailbox as my eyes catch sight of what's ahead of me, and I freeze. A glimpse of someone getting into a green SUV and Penn was aiming straight towards it. I watch Penn follow it out of the neighborhood until both the mysterious SUV and dragon are out of sight.

I continue my walk down to the mailbox and take out my key and unlock it to see a journal with a new pen stacked on top of the mail. I grab everything that was in there and lock the mailbox back up before looking down at Scooby.

"Alright, we gotta head home, Scooby," I say, placing everything in my messenger bag. "Our job here is done."

Back at the house, I let Scooby off his leash and he pads off to his bed. Poor boy, he hates going to the mailbox because I make him walk the hill with me. I put the regular mail on the dining table and head to my bedroom. I place the pen down on my

Leah Silverwhisp

desk and open up the journal to see a single oracle card, *Scots Pine*. On the page behind the card, I see the familiar handwriting that read to signify clarity, a new perspective, and new beginnings.

I close the journal and place it next to the pen, then pull out the dragon pendant from my pocket. Time to see, what you are up to, Shev. My bed becomes my meditation spot as I make myself comfortable while holding the pendant in my hands, focusing on Penn and looking through its eyes. It's as if I were adjusting a camera lens, carefully syncing myself up to my little dragon as the images before me become clearer.

There in a small office filled with boxes sat a man with a strong powerful presence. He definitely resembles of a Viking that very well could be the god of lightning. Yet, when I meet his piercing green eyes which look right back onto me, I feel my heart skip a beat. Shev smirks, then scribbles something down on his desk before holding it up for me to see. There on his note pad is a note written in his handwriting:

Leah Silverwhisp

Hello, my darling, Haili.

My eyes flow open, losing the connection. I sit up and clutch the pendant. This may – may not work. Shev knows. Of course he knows. Why did I fool myself into thinking that he would not know? Now, I have to try something else, something unexpected that will catch him off guard. Should I try to connect with Penn again? I clutch the pendant and close my eyes again trying to focus on Penn. Just a little adjustment and I'm back to viewing Shev's boxed up office space, but what I see is truly unbelievable— Penn happily eating an apple out of his hand.

Seriously, Penn! You little traitor. Well, maybe that is an overreaction. Penn could be just hungry, and Shev is kind enough to feed it. Nope, that smirk says it all. The minute he showed me the note, no, the minute I saw him pull away from the mailbox. Should I just surrender and be pampered like Penn because he seems to be winning the game right now? At this rate, I am going to have to take it up a notch and keep an eye on both Penn and Shev.

Leah Silverwhisp

Alright, Shev, two can play this game of yours. You think you're cute with your little tricks and feeding my dragon. I can make you crazy too and you will have to make a move.

I flip open my laptop and phone, unsure if he has actually found a way to hack into my electronics or not. But in case he did, I snap my fingers triggering the voice recorder inside the stuffed wolf to play. My cheeks flush as I hear the sound of his voice.

I pick up one of my leather journals and flip it open to a random page. The heat in my face grows hotter as I read one of my foolish hardy rants about him. Ugh! This is his fault! I glare at the cameras facing me from the desk. I rub my face trying to relieve the embarrassment that I have forced upon myself. I look around the room, what else could I do? There's a book on my bed. A book in my purse. A book on my desk. A book in front of my TV. I pull the book out of my purse and open it to a spicy page as my face flushes brighter as I contemplate about reading this out loud.

Leah Silverwhisp

Nope. No – no – no – no. As much as I enjoy a good spicy read, I can't. The fact that my parents might hear me. I hide my face in the book. Nope. Can't happen. A sudden spell of weakness hits me and my knees buckle causing me to fall to the floor. The book in my hand falls closing shut as I let out a heavy breath. Crack! Ow! I bite my lips hard holding back a cry. My trembling hand pulls up my tank top to reveal a purple patch on my skin starting to form. Crack! Snap! I quickly grab one of my leather belts that I have lying on the floor and bite down on it.

Pain crackles all over my body as tears stream down my face blurring my vision. Snap! The taste of leather fills my mouth as I bite down harder. Something foreign yet familiar scoops me up. My eyes sting with tears as pain continues to ripple throughout my body. I cry grasping at my clothes trying to tear them off my body. I am too hot for these damn things!

The leather belt starts to get a new hole as my canines pierce it from my struggles in a stranger's arms, finally freeing myself from

118

Leah Silverwhisp

my tank top as they place me in the back of a very spacious car. Pain courses through my body as I hear the door close and another door opens and closes. Crack! Snap! Pop! I should probably care that I am being kidnapped right now but... Ow! Pop! Why does it feel like my insides are stabbing me with sharp pointy sticks? Wait. No. Nope. Ow! Don't think about it – don't think about the tiny needles of bone that are splintering throughout your body right now – don't think about the throbbing sensation of your bones expanding and shrinking repeatedly as they grow – don't think about how your blood has now become lava – don't think about what is happening. I plead with myself, but that's all I can focus on. Nothing, but the pain.

Leah Silverwhisp

Shevaron: Round 3

After I leave the community with Haili's little spy, I bring it into my office and work at my desk. Penn watches me closely, while I keep an eye on it until its little yellow eyes turn blue. I meet those pretty blue eyes and write a little note on my note pad to show the little dragon, or should I say Haili who's now watching me work at my desk. Penn's eyes quickly turn golden causing a chuckle to escape my throat.

I break the apple Owen left for me on my desk apart into slices using my claws. The apple's juices coat my hands as I hold the slices of apple baiting the little spy over with a tasty snack. Penn lands near me and sniffs the apple before eating it happily. Penn's eyes once again turn blue as its tail and wings twitch. For a moment, they stay blue but soon return to gold.

I glance over at my laptop screen that now has Haili's bedroom in view from two screens. What is she doing? I place the apple slices down and freeze. Haili snaps her fingers and plays the recording I have left

120

her. Her face flushes bright red as it plays. I should leave her more voice messages, I want her to make that face all the time, fuck. Haili picks up a journal and reads it quietly to herself, her face turning redder by the second. No one should be this cute. What the hell is in that book? I need to know.

Suddenly, I grab my phone and keeping the live feed going, I get back in the SUV and head to see Haili despite how late it is. I should really get a car of my own. I pull out onto the road and head towards the community. Not sure how fast I am going, but once I reach the community, I slow down and drive up to *our* house. As I park, a thud sounding from my phone catches my attention and I look down to see Haili has collapsed to the ground.

My heart skips a beat as her trembling hands struggle to pull up her tank top to reveal a purple spot starting to form around her ribs. Fuck. I scramble out of the SUV and enter her parents' house. I don't have time to explain why I am here or what is happening to their daughter. They turn from the TV to look at me in shock when I come

121

Leah Silverwhisp

in. I quickly apologize and do what I did for Jack all those years ago. I take out the matching talisman I gave Haili and activate its magick.

Her parents blink a couple of times, looking confused and go back to watching TV. I hurry into Haili's room to see her reaching for her belt that was discarded on the floor. She bites down on it trying not to alert her parents in the next room. I scoop her up and activate her talisman. I hold her close to my chest and carry her out of the house without anyone noticing. She starts to struggle in my arms, trying to tear her clothes off and finally succeeding when I place her in the back of Selene's SUV.

I quickly close the door and get into the driver's seat. I start driving and head towards the nearest mountains. GPS says it's at least 15 minutes away from where we are. I glance at Haili at the back as she tries to muffle her cries by biting down on the belt. I have to get her deep into the mountains. My foot presses down on the gas pedal speeding down the road until we reach the base of the

Leah Silverwhisp

mountains. I quickly park the SUV and get out.

I open the back door and scoop Haili up as she winces in my arms, her blood drenching my shirt. A sickening feeling fills my heart as guilt hits me hard with reality. Her pain is my fault, Haili's bruised and bloody body in my arms as I hold her princess style. I pull her close kissing the top of her head before making a beeline for the tree line and away from the man-made trails.

Once we reach the tree line, my instincts take over as I begin navigating the trees going deeper into the mountains away from society. Haili holds her mouth down on the piece of belt until she can't anymore. The belt falls away from her mouth as she cries out loudly in pain. By now, Haili has reached the worst part. She pushes off from me and quickly unhooks her bra, kicking off her jeans with her panties.

Haili stands up for a moment as she leans against me, her naked body covered in bruises and blood. She collapses onto the ground crying out loudly as her body jolts

123

Leah Silverwhisp

violently. Her bones begin cracking and snapping more frequently.

Carefully, I kneel next to her. "Haili," I say calmly even though my heart is ripping me a new one for causing her this much pain. "I'm right here, I'm not going anywhere. I need you to listen to me and breathe, the more that you fight it, the worse it will be. Can you do that?"

She nods. That's a good sign.

"Breathe and let it happen. I'm not going anywhere. Don't hold anything back."

Haili cries out in pain as her back arches and more bruises form over old ones. "Shev," she breathes out my name. "I believe I told you that the minute your game ends, mine begins." Her beautiful blue eyes meet mine. "Get ready to run, wolf boy."

Leah Silverwhisp

Haili: Spindle

Yep, I still plan to make him work for it. Ow! Bloody hell, what happened to my high pain tolerance? Why is the back part worse, is it because that's my most sensitive and ticklish spot? Probably, ow! No, not the worst! I cry out in pain as I feel like someone took a sledgehammer to my face. I glance over at Shev, whose eyes are filled with concern and guilt as he watches over me. My teasing didn't help relieve his stress. A sharp jagged pain shoots through my back and into my skull and another followed by several. I cry out and try to breathe, my mind spins as all matter of thoughts blur and mush together.

My vision blurs distorting the colors into dark globs as the pain becomes unbearable to the point of stopping all my thoughts in their tracks. The only thing left is a wild urge that claws its way out of me. It claws away at my insides, tearing away at my consciousness and flooding my thoughts.

For a few moments, I see nothing and feel a killer headache coming on, while my body

125

Leah Silverwhisp

throbs from the inside out. When trying to suppress the headache and seeing if I have accidentally caught a fever, a fuzzy brown paw comes into my field of vision. A paw?

The taste of leather clung to the insides of my mouth overwhelms my tastebuds as I spin around looking for the belt. There just a few feet away it lays on the ground. It no longer resembles a belt, though. Multiple holes have been pierced through it and is now stained in blood. Oops, think I kind of turned that into Swiss cheese or a ruined chew toy that was once a collar.

A groan escapes deep within my throat turning into a growl. My headache grows worse with every sound as everything in the mountains becomes amplified. The busy little ants stomping their way to their ant hills. Birds chirping like dead fricken smoke alarms. Leaves swishing mockingly at the scene below them. A clever sneaky fox killing a poor little bunny rabbit just a few yards away. The bunny rabbit's squeals driving my headache into overdrive.

Leah Silverwhisp

I take a deep breath and close my eyes trying to focus on just a singular sound, a singular presence that isn't the sheer amount of pain I am in nor the overwhelming amount of sensory knowledge that is slamming into my brain. Finally, I hear it. A single sound, a single familiar presence.

At first, it's a slowing heartbeat that isn't my own followed by a steady rhythm of someone breathing near me. A familiar, yet calming presence that my soul has known and never seen for years.

"Haili," Shev says to me through the soul connect. His voice as tempting as ever.

"Shev," I answer as I turn to face him. He seems to be bigger than I imagined, now that I have got to have a good look at him. Or am I just this short? I must have shrunk! Damn, my body feels as though someone filled me with sand or maybe lead. Was I hit by a truck or something? Jeez.

A gentle cool breeze brushes up against my... skin? No, it feels different. A little shiver as I wiggle my body, wait, no. Am I standing on all fours? I title my head in all

Leah Silverwhisp

directions trying to see myself and embarrassingly chasing my new fluffy light brown fur. News alert, channel 4 everyone! I have a tail and it's fluffy.

After a moment of embarrassingly confirming that I am indeed a wolf and I haven't lost my mind—though that could change if I keep chasing my tail like an excited puppy—I look back at Shev as my fluffy tail begins to sway. Should I tackle him? I feel like I should tackle him and make the playing ground even. You know, he has had the advantage this entire time and he even saw me without my shirt on.

I could make him shirtless too, I think to myself. No. Too dangerous, I'll lose so fast, and I haven't even begun my game. Best to stick with the plan and make him work for it.

"Catch me if you can," I tease before taking off running deeper into the mountains.

My limbs ache, heart pumps, and oh boy was I ready to run. The wind up against my fur feels so good as a cooling sensation

128

Leah Silverwhisp

rushes up against me. If I stayed back there, I would have most definitely tried to remove Shev's bloodied shirt and lose the game. I would have tackled him to the ground and licked his cheeky grin before he took control. Stop thinking, Haili. Just run. If your mind ends up in the gutter again, your instincts to turn back and lose on purpose will take over.

A playful yet familiar growl sounds somewhere behind. Then a powerful piercing howl that reaches my heart and soul. My adrenaline increases as I run faster. Run. Run like you just scratched Dean's impala or ate his pie. Run and don't stop.

The pain is finally subsiding too, thank the universe for that. I can think clearly for once without a throbbing headache. You know what I just realized, my soul has been bursting with joy this entire time and I am only now just feeling the lightness of what the feeling of joy brings. Never have I felt so free, so fulfilled, and so much joy.

A flash of silver leaps over me and stops me in my tracks. Right in front of me, a

129

Leah Silverwhisp

massive gray wolf. I slowly back away. I am not done making him chase me. My tail sways as I lean down close to the earth and then launch myself forward running straight for him and leap over him.

My landing isn't graceful at all, his wolf form being so much bigger than mine. I stumble and smack myself into a nearby tree. Ow. I push myself back up stumbling back into the run. Fast and hard my feet pound into the ground.

A deep chuckle in my head followed by a playful growl. *"Haili, do you really think you can outrun me?"*

Leah Silverwhisp

Shevaron: Soul Connection

Oh, she truly thinks she can outrun me. *How long should I play with her before I claim my prize?* I think to myself as I chase after her. Our eternal connection is just too strong, and I can hear every thought she has, including how badly she secretly wanted to tear my shirt off me and pin me to the ground. Missed opportunities. Luckily for me, I can win at any time and when I do, I'll keep my word too.

I chase after the fluff of her tail, weaving in and out of the trees as I pick up the pace. I go through several options in how I'll end our little game. Option one, I could nip her but causing her to jump up just enough for me to knock her off her feet and pin her to the ground. Then we have option number two, I straight on tackle her into the ground and lick her face. Lastly, option number three I do both options.

Just a little faster and a small nip at her flank causing her to yelp and jump as I use my body weight to throw her off her balance and tackle her to the ground. Another small

Leah Silverwhisp

nip at her neck. She yelps and squirms trying to break free, but I keep her pinned.

"Sorry, darling, but do you know how long I waited for this day?" I say, licking her snout playfully.

A small whimper escapes her as she looks up at me. *"Because you chose to wait."* She pouts mentally.

"For your own good." I grind up against her as I keep her pinned beneath me. *"Now are you going to be a good girl and let me claim my prize or do I have to bite you into submission?"*

She whimpers again and tries to push off, but I am much bigger than her wolf form. Haili lets out a couple of growls in frustration trying to find a way out of this. The best part about it is her thoughts, feelings, and her desperate attempt to be in control when every instinct is telling her to the exact opposite.

It makes me chuckle and I grind against her again as another wave of her thoughts and feelings washes over me. *I'm so*

Leah Silverwhisp

doomed, she thinks as I grind against her. My cock teasing her causes her to squirm. She begs me to shove it inside. So, I do. She yelps out in pain and begs me to go harder. Her fantasies excite me as I begin to actually tease her entrance with my hardened wolf cock. Her eyes widen in realization and she growls at me.

I tease her entrance more causing her to whimper again. *"Not my fault, your thoughts are your own."*

"Are they?" she asks, trying to keep her composure. *Damnit, Shev, stop teasing me already,* her thoughts growl.

"Yes, I just get to hear how badly you want me," I say teasingly as I lean down and nip her neck. She whimpers as her composure slips again.

I stop teasing her and slide myself all the way in, inch by inch. My thrusts are getting faster and faster as she begs me to not hold back.

"Just claim me as the winner and I will gladly obey your thoughts, darling," I tease

Leah Silverwhisp

her playfully as I continue to tease her entrance.

She growls up at me and whimpers as I keep her pinned, knowing very well that there's no escape. Our mate connection wasn't just that of soul mates; we are eternal flames. Every time we connect, our souls ignite into a brilliant ray of colors that neither of us could escape. Years of soul connecting with each other, that much was obvious.

Haili growls again, *"You made me wait, why should I let you win?"*

I bite her neck gently causing another whimper to escape her throat. *"You know exactly why I made you wait,"* I say as I press my body against hers.

She grunts at me and huffs, *"You made me wait since I turned nineteen years old, Shev. Twenty-one years of waiting,"* Haili elaborates. *"Give me a better reason to why I should let you win?"*

Okay, fair point. *"Haili, the main reason why I waited was for you to live a happy*

134

Leah Silverwhisp

normal life with your family and achieve your dreams without my interference causing you to shift. Also, the very thought of you being in pain because of me," I say, looking into her beautiful blue eyes. *"Especially, that kind of pain."*

Haili says nothing for a moment, she knows I have a point. Whether she likes it or not, her waiting all these years has been for her own good. For a moment, she remains silent as I wait for her response. Not budging an inch until she caves.

"You know technically, I won your game, and you won mine," she finally says with a spark of wildfire in her eyes.

And at that moment, I fall for her all over again. Every single time she gets that spark in her eyes, I fall for her more. *"Oh, really you think you won my game?"*

She licks my face. *"Yes, otherwise I wouldn't be here, Shev. You caved first,"* Haili says matter-of-factly.

Damnit, why does she have to be so darn cute when she is right? Her last move had

135

Leah Silverwhisp

me drive straight over there as she teased me with her many cute facial expressions that I completely blanked on the radius rule and ended up causing her to start shifting early. Haili had won the very second I arrived in front of her parents' ranch style house.

Haili nips at me, and I snap out of thoughts to see a confident smug look in her eyes. *"Say it,"* she dares me.

I nip back at her and bite her again. I'll bite her into submission later. For now, though, I look at her as she waits for me to admit it. I hear the swishing of her tail on the ground. *"I lost first,"* I grumble. *"You won."*

"Thank you." She licks me again. *"I lost my game, so I guess you won too,"* Haili teases, clearly enjoying this.

I push my way into her causing her to yelp as I catch her off guard. Inch by inch, I push myself deeper inside of her as a whimper escapes her throat.

"Shev," Haili gasps, letting out a pained moan.

Leah Silverwhisp

My thrusts are slow and steady at first. Haili winces every now and then, her body still a little bit sore and hot from the shift. I bite at her neck again as I feel her tightening around me. My hips move deeper inside of her. I slowly pull out of her before pushing myself back in.

"Haili," I grunt as I slide all the way into her tight wet pussy.

I start moving my hips faster, pounding inside of her as my cock reaches deep inside. Haili moans louder in my mind. Instinctively, I pound harder as she starts to squirm against me.

Another bite. "Keep still," I growl into her neck causing her to whimper as she tightens up even more.

I nip at her and thank the universe that it wasn't a full moon, otherwise I wouldn't be able to do this. In a last spurt of energy, I pound Haili hard and bite her neck causing her to cum on my cock making me go even deeper. My cum erupts deep inside of her as she reverts back to human form before passing out.

Leah Silverwhisp

Haili: Willow

I wake up to the sunlight coming through the windows of an unfamiliar car, yet the set strong scent of my blood says otherwise. The heat rushes to my face as I recall what happened in the mountains. Did I just sleep with Shev? As a wolf? Oh boy, I really do have a biting kink and a defiant brat kink.

My body aches all over as I carefully move and feel something sticky in between my legs, which inspires me to examine the rest of my body. No discoloring skin of any sort. No broken bones. No scars. A whole bunch of bite marks on my neck. I touch them, looking at the rearview mirror. Several reddish rings have formed there, including smaller marks of when he nipped me. I notice the talisman still around my neck, when I hear a knock on the car window.

"I have a spare set of clothes inside the duffle bag," Shev's voice says from outside the car.

Leah Silverwhisp

I look down at a black duffle bag and unzip it as I feel my face scrunch up. "You seriously expect me to wear this?"

"It's that or I take you home naked," he says, leaning up against the SUV.

I grumble as I pull on a baggy pink sweatshirt and black leggings, then suddenly open the door causing him to stumble forward. "Whose clothes are these?"

"My beta's mate Selene's, it's her SUV that I am using," he says simply.

I nod and try not to cringe at the pink. "Remind me to thank her later."

"It can't be that bad," he teases as he opens the passenger door for me.

Without a word, I hop into the passenger seat and fold my arms. "At least it's better than white."

"No, that would be Jack's favorite color." She chuckles and closes the door.

Shev gets into the driver's seat. He turns to look at me and I see the corners of his lips

Leah Silverwhisp

up turn into a smirk. "You do look good in pink, though."

My eyes roll. "Don't make me bite you."

He chuckles and leans in to kiss me deeply. "Maybe some other time, but for now, I have to take you home and let the magic recharge in the talismans."

I press my lips up against his and bite his lip playfully. "Not yet. I have questions and you have the answers."

Shev looks at me carefully and looks as if he was calculating something in his head. I understood there was time and a place for everything, but right now I am incredibly hungry, and I absolutely refuse to let this end this way. Our games may be over, but I just shifted into a wolf for the first time and slept with him in my wolf form. By no means, is he just going to drop me off and stop this game of tag.

"Haili," Shev says seriously, looking pained for what he is about to say. "The talismans are running out of time, which means I have to take you straight home

Leah Silverwhisp

before your parents realize you have been gone all night."

He starts driving the car out of the parking lot and heads in the direction of home. Damnit, Shev, I wanted to have this conversation in person and not in my head for once. "Fine," I say, my voice coming out a bit more annoyed than expected. "You owe me a day. A full day of us actually talking about everything."

Shev keeps his eyes on the road. "Are you asking me out on a date, darling?"

I growl as he teases me. I'm going to bite him later for that. "Yes, if you are dropping me off after you slept with me. Then yes, I'm asking you out on a date."

"Then ask me," he teases again. "Before we get to your house."

Bite him hard. "Will you – go on – a date with me – this Friday?"

"All day?" he asks with a playful grin on his lips.

"Yes, all day."

"You do know what that means," he teases.

My face flushes as I recall him pinning me down in his wolf form. "No fun until we talk."

"I'll pick you up at 11 a.m.," Shev says as he drives down the road.

After a short bit of driving, he pulls up into the neighborhood and drives down the different blocks until we arrive in front of *our home*. "Alright, darling. Once you're back inside your room, you can escape the pink and turn off the talisman. Don't worry about your parents; the talisman is imbued with fey magic and charms anyone who knows you to momentarily forget about you. So, it will be like you never left."

"What about you?" I ask, not budging from my seat.

He pulls out his own talisman from under his shirt. "They won't remember me walking into your house and startling them. My talisman has a bit of an extra kick."

I turn to look at him and his talisman. Okay, that answered some of my questions

Leah Silverwhisp

to how he managed to get me without rising any suspicion. "My clothes," I say. "What about my clothes and my belt?"

"I plan to give them back to you on Friday. I will have to replace the belt, though, you kind of destroyed it," Shev teases as he leans in to kiss me. "Now, go inside before I change my mind and keep you for myself."

My lips press back into his as I look into his warm green eyes. "Fine, but I still have questions."

"I know," he says, pressing his forehead against mine. "I will answer any questions you have on Friday, I promise."

After a short moment of hesitation, I leave the car and head back into the house. Scooby follows me into my bedroom. I close the door and strip off the pink sweater and leggings, switching into my own set of comfy clothes for when I lounge around the house. Scooby watches me carefully as I turn off the talisman. I place a finger to my lips and whisper to Scooby, "Our little secret."

143

Leah Silverwhisp

Shevaron: Revolutionaries

I force myself to drive away and head back to the rental home, where I find Selene and Owen wait in the driveway for me. Something isn't right, their expressions seem grim. Carefully, I pull up into the driveway and get out of the SUV. Owen is the first to move as he approaches me and places his hand on my shoulder whispering in my ear, "Jack was attacked."

My heart skips a beat; I look at Owen then to Selene. "Where is he?"

"In his room resting," she says as I start for the house.

"Shev," she says quietly.

I don't stay to hear the rest of it. Instead, I stumble through the house until I find Jack 'resting' in his bed. Jack sits up in his bed with bandages around his gut and his arm in a sling, while using his uninjured hand to type away fast on his computer like a man possessed. He doesn't even notice me coming into the room.

144

"Jack," I say as I near him carefully.

"They took her," he says flatly as he smashes away his keyboard. He doesn't even look up.

"Who did they take, Jack?" I ask him softly as he grits his teeth in frustration at the computer screen.

"They took Emmy," he growls and types faster. "Come on, you cowards, stop hiding and make your move."

Oh shit. Jack might have soul connected with his charge. His desperate expression and obsessive focus said it all. Even her nickname gave it away. I'm not sure if he realizes it yet. An alarm suddenly sounds from my office down the hallway as my phone buzzes with a message from Owen:

They are going after everyone.

I run to my office and see Haili wielding her staff against two intruders. How is this possible, I just dropped her off. Haili knocks one of them down and holds the other one down with her foot. She has kept her parents and Scooby safe as the two intruders run out her bedroom door, and she casts a protective ward around her bedroom.

"Haili, stay in there," I tell her pleadingly.

She shakes her head and heads towards the bedroom door. Damnit, Haili, listen to me. *"They are after me, right?"* she asks, standing at the threshold.

"Yes," I admit as she places her hand on the door handle.

She nods and opens the fricken door and leaves her room. Then quickly closes it behind her. *"Fill me in,"* she says.

I growl in frustration and text Owen back:

Get everyone back here and make the calls.

Selene is already on it. You left the keys in the ignition. Do you want her to grab Haili too?

"Shev," Haili says a little out of breath. *"Fill me in."*

"They are grabbing any shifters born around your birthday because of the veil

146

thinning. Just a group of frustrated supernaturals that see a chance to flip the world on its head and hope that will fix everyone's problems."

"Did they take anyone?" she asks, sounding more out of breath. I can feel her energy dwindling, which means she is running out of magick.

I grip my phone and text:

Haili is in the middle of fighting them right now.

Oh shit.

Have Selene return with everyone first. If we face them, we face them together.

"Yes, they took someone already. Now will you please return to your room and hide until I can get there?"

A silent pause as I feel a strange sense of resolve wash over her. No, Haili, don't you do it. All of her energy is suddenly depleted. Another moment of silence passes and another.

"Haili!" No response. *"Haili please."*

147

"I don't suppose, you have a clean-up crew," she finally says, sounding completely exhausted.

"What did do you?" I say as I head downstairs and find Owen contacting our allies in Vermont.

Haili's energy is coming back slowly. *"I bought you time by taking out the first wave."*

"First wave," my voice growls.

"Yeah, I kinda challenged them too by sending them a message," she says innocently.

I palm my face as Owen looks over at me with a questioning look. *"What was your exact message?"*

A small pause of silence. *"Um, I said something along the lines of let's play a game of capture flag. Bring your captives and try to capture me before I set them free."*

Leah Silverwhisp

I grab one of Selene's note pads and pens scribbling down a note for Owen to read while he is on the phone:

Haili has challenged them, get ready to leave.

Owen reads the message and nods before filling in our allies on the other end of the phone. A loud thud sounds from upstairs as I hear Jack's pained growls come down the stairs. I signal Owen to get off his phone and help me with Jack as I nudge my head towards the stairs. He looks up the stairs and finishes his phone call before hanging up.

"Should I tell him or will you?" Owen says as he approaches the stairs.

I look at Owen as we hear a mumble of curse words sounding off in the distance. "Together," I say and then pause almost forgetting to respond back to Haili. *"Get back in your room and stay put until I get there."*

"Fine."

Owen and I head upstairs to see Jack struggling to put his clothes on. We both

149

Leah Silverwhisp

sigh and walk over to Jack who growls at us. "Don't try to stop me," he says as his bandage starts to bleed again. "I have to rescue Emmy."

I clap my hands loudly causing him to sit down abruptly so Owen can replace his bandages as I look at Jack dead in the eyes. "I'm not going to stop you. In fact, we are here to tell you something very important that will help you. However, we can't do that if you pass out from blood loss."

Jack glares at me and nods. "Fine, but make it quick."

I look at Owen who has finished replacing Jack's bandages. "We are going to teach you the ultimate hack, a hack that only you can do."

"Really, right now," he says, trying to stand up, but Owen pushes him right back down. "Why do I need both of – you?" He stares at us now. "Impossible."

"The first time it happened to Shev it was years ago, before you joined the pack and the timing couldn't be worse," Owen says, recalling the day that my father's pack was attacked.

"I shifted for the first time," I say as I force those buried memories to resurface. "Everything happened so fast. A rogue wolf pack attacked, and their leader killed my father who was Alpha at the time and forced himself onto my mother. Out of pure adrenaline from what was happening around me, I had shifted and started fighting my way through every rogue wolf I came upon. When I finally reached my parents, my father was dead, and my mom lay there broken."

"He was by no means, in shape to take on a rogue alpha wolf by himself," Owen adds. "However, a little voice inside of his head changed everything."

"In that moment, Haili was the one who connected to me first without realizing it," I continue. "All she said was *I feel like I should write something profound, but all I can say is that if you are out there and this somehow gets through to you, then I have only one thing to tell you. Good luck and*

151

Leah Silverwhisp

don't do anything that you will regret later.'
And that seemed to calm me down enough
to analyze my surroundings and call for
backup as Owen came rushing in with the
rest of the pack and together, we took down
the rogue alpha."

"Thank the universe for Haili soul
connecting with you then. Otherwise, you
might be dead alongside your parents and
would leave me with all the clean-up work,"
Owen says as Selene honks the horn.

Jack sighs in defeat and looks over at
Owen. "When did your soul connection
happen?"

"That is a story for another time, but for
now rest and run communications. We will
go get your girl and make sure she is safe,"
Owen says and gets up, then runs out of the
room to get into the SUV with the others.

"How do you connect with Haili," Jack
asks me softly as I turn to leave.

"By simply thinking about her," I say and
think about the first time I responded to her.
"Just think about talking to her and it will

Leah Silverwhisp

happen, eventually. Though she may
question her sanity," I tease before leaving
the room and joining the others.

Haili: Dragon

I disobey Shev's request to go back to my room. I need to replenish my energy, I'm starving. I walk over to the pantry and pull out the brown sugar, flour, chocolate chips and cinnamon. Then I grab the eggs and oat milk from the fridge. A stainless-steel bowl from the cabinet. Three cracked eggs and some guess work later and I have made a nice creamy pancake batter and oiled the frying pan before dropping the first spoonful of batter into the center. I watch it bubble as I hum to a random song in my head, then flip it over.

One pancake, two pancakes, flip, three pancakes, flip, munch! I repeat this process until I have a whole stack of chocolate chip pancakes with a partially eaten one. I turn off the stove and let the pan cool. I sit at the dining room table as I enjoy my stack of pancakes.

A couple of moments pass, and Shev arrives with what I assume to be his pack. He walks into the dining room and freezes at

Leah Silverwhisp

the sight of me eating pancakes. A man in a black T-shirt walks over and asks, "May I?"

"Help yourself," I say, sliding over the stack of pancakes.

He picks one up and takes a bite as Shev looks at me. "I thought I told you to go back into your room and wait for me. Not make yourself *motivational pancakes* after antagonizing the enemy."

"These are really good," Owen exclaims and shares them with a woman who is wearing a cute pink sweater.

"Not my fault somebody didn't listen to me first, when I said I was hungry this morning and didn't take me out to eat breakfast. Then after said somebody dropped me off and I just got into my comfortable clothes. These guys," I point to the two supernaturals laid out cold in the center of the living room with duct tape binding their limbs, "came barging in and spooked poor Scooby and my parents so bad that I had to reveal myself and use the last of my energy to buy us time." I take a couple

155

Leah Silverwhisp

of more bites of the pancake in my hand. "I needed to replenish my energy somehow."

"And you decided on *motivational pancakes,*" Shev says, shaking his head.

"Yes, we are about to engage in a battle and rescue someone," I say proudly as I take another bite of my pancakes feeling my energy return. "It's the perfect time for them."

"What makes them motivational pancakes," asks the woman in the pink sweater, which I assume is Selene from the clothes I borrowed this morning.

"I think I started calling them that when I knew I had to get homework done and wasn't in the right mindset for it. So, I would motivate myself by making pancakes and it kind of became a thing," I explain.

"Oh, that is why you had Owen teach you," Selene says to Shev as she wolfs a pancake down.

Unfortunately, all conversations halt as the sounds of tires and agitated voices come from outside. Our guests have finally

156

arrived. Shev turns to look at me. "Bedroom, now."

"No," I refuse before wolfing down another pancake.

Shev walks over to me. "Don't argue with me and just get in there, we will handle this."

I grab my staff that was leaning up against the fridge and tap it on the floor, "Seppherian, wake up and come out."

A green scaled dragon with brownish hues emerges from the staff, standing to the same size as Shev's massive wolf form. I pat her head and glance over at the group as a bunch of crackling sounds start to sound from my bedroom and even Penn Craft appears in the hallway with an army of dragons that are slowly increasing in size.

"Enchanting?" Shev asks, looking at me.

I continue to pet Seppherian as he waits for me to respond. "Yep," I say, holding out my hand as the smaller dragons become pieces of armor on me.

157

Leah Silverwhisp

"I don't want to know why you have so many," Shev says, shaking his head as the front door rattles.

"You already know," I say with a smile, kissing him. "I was bored and tired of waiting for you and seemed like no matter what I did, you were dead set on staying away from me because it was for my own good. However, I wasn't just going to sit and wait for you to come anymore, so while you played keep away, I rooted myself in my schoolwork and studied hard, while practicing magic on the side. Over the course of time, I may have enchanted over a dozen dragons."

The first revolutionary barges in by breaking through the window as I point my staff at him and shoot a gust of wind sending him flying into their unmarked white van. More of them start piling in, and Seppherian flaps her wings to push them back with short bursts of wind. Shev and his pack get to work too by subduing the others that were coming from the back door. After a while of knocking them around with gusts of wind, I hear a bunch of violent growls and grunts

Leah Silverwhisp

coming from behind me. I sigh deeply as I rafiki-chop one of them in the head knocking them out cold. Time to end things I guess, otherwise my pancakes will get cold and weird.

Seppherian and I sync up as I bring my staff back steadily, with it pointing around the room. I release the staff and send it flying around the room knocking all the revolutionaries out cold on the floor. I signal my dragons with my staff to pile them up in the middle of the living room as I contemplate if I should let my dragons chow down. Penn Craft, being the only dragon unaccounted for, has slipped outside and checks the unmarked van to see a frightened girl on the inside.

I clean off the table and check on the pancakes. Okay, good they are still warm and there's no broken glass in them. Thank you, Seppherian, for making sure of that. I pick up the plate and head outside of the house, ordering Penn Craft to open the van's door. Penn pulls the door open to reveal the frightened young woman hugging her knees with tears soaking her face.

159

Leah Silverwhisp

"Hey," I say sweetly. "Do you want some pancakes? I happened to make too much and can't eat them by myself."

She nods and rubs her face before leaving the van. Together, we sit down on the front lawn and just take in the view of the unfinished house in front of us. Once she finishes eating, she puts the plate down next to her.

"I've been hearing this strange guy in my head," she admits out loud to me. "I feel like I am losing my mind. Maybe I am, why else would I see shifters and dragons fighting in front of an ordinary house? No one else seems to even notice what is going on."

"Believe me, I have been asking myself the very same question for years," I say as I feel Shev step out of the house watching me closely. "But I can tell you one thing for sure, that voice inside your head feels different, doesn't it?"

She nods. "It feels like my soul has turned into the sun all of the sudden."

160

Leah Silverwhisp

"Then you have nothing to worry about," I say, standing up and stretching out my arms as I command my dragons to restore everything around us as if nothing has happened. "Just don't wait for things to happen." I turn to look at Shev and smile. "Destiny has its way of working things out, but that doesn't mean you can't shake it a little bit and have some fun along the way."

Leah Silverwhisp

Shevaron: Motivational Pancakes

After the whole ordeal and clean-up in July, everything went back to normal and I had to postpone the date with Haili as she was finishing her summer classes, while I had to focus on paperwork for the pack. September has finally rolled in, and both houses are now move-in ready, which means that I can finally get back to the original plan of moving everyone in and dealing with a stir-crazy Jack who doesn't know what to do with himself. Fortunately, for him he doesn't have to worry about running a pack or how to handle his eternal soul connection because he has me and Owen to walk him through everything. Selene too, though she mostly teases the crap out of him.

Haili also has had her hands full because she revealed herself to her parents and had to explain everything to them, including the fact that I may have been borderline stalking her and communicating with her over the years. Needless to say, they were in denial at first but couldn't explain the strange

162

Leah Silverwhisp

happenings or how their daughter's dragon collection came to life in her room. Though after some long conversations and visible proof, they came to an understanding of why Haili has kept it on the downlow for so long.

I am unpacking the boxes in the new house, when Haili walks in through the front door carrying a stack of pancakes. "I made you some motivational pancakes." She beams with a playful smile.

One glance at those pancakes and I walk over to her, scooping her up as I grab the plate of pancakes. I carry them both into the bedroom and put the pancakes on the night table after tossing Haili down onto the bed. Then I climb over as I pull off her clothes and replace them with the pancakes from her plate. I carefully line them up with her breasts all the way down to her pussy and then bind her hands with the own bra. I use my legs to spread hers apart.

"If only I had some whipped cream," I say as Penn Craft flies in with a can and places it next to her.

Leah Silverwhisp

"You little traitor," Haili gasps as I waste no time to cover her in whipped cream.

"Now these are motivational pancakes," I tease her as I lean down and bite one of the pancakes that rests on her breast causing her to let out a small yelp. I lick my lips and bite her breast again as I take another piece of the pancake. "I'm feeling so motivated right now."

She yelps again and whimpers as I finish cleaning her breast with my tongue and bite her nipple. I continue to eat my way down her body, leaving bite marks on her breasts and stomach. I eat the last pancake carefully and teasingly as my teeth graze her clit causing her to squirm. I lick her pussy clean and bite gently causing her back to arch off the bed.

"Shev," she gasps as she looks down at me. "Is this about what happened two months ago?"

I lick up her body biting and nipping at her until I meet her lips. Her bottom lip tastes like strawberries as I bite it playfully while looking into her eyes hungrily. "One of the reasons, you clearly disobeyed me and this is your punishment." I bite down on her neck causing her to gasp loudly.

"What is the other reason?" She squirms as I keep her pinned.

"You went ahead and published the book without me reading it first." I lick the spot where I bit her causing her to moan. "And I always keep my word. You are not leaving this room until I bite you into submission."

She leans her head back as I bite and nip down her body and spray more whipped cream onto her pussy. I start eating her out as she moans out my name. Haili squirms as I growl for her to keep still. She whimpers. I bite her inner thigh and go back to eating her out causing her to orgasm as she arches her back again. Her body collapses back onto the bed as I slide off my underwear and crawl over her as she pants.

"Are you going to behave and stop being stubborn?" I say as I press my cock against her pussy.

Leah Silverwhisp

"You know, Jack told me I connected with you first and I clearly remember that day I wrote in my journal," she breathes as her blue eyes find mine, *"Good luck and don't do anything that you will regret later.* I stand by these words."

I shove myself inside of her and grin mischievously. "It's going to be a long day for you then, darling."

Haili gasps loudly arching her back as I start moving roughly against her. Her body is covered in bitemarks and what remains of the whipped cream. I lean over her and kiss her deeply, my pace never slowing down. Her moans vibrate against my lips as I thrust deep into her, and I look at her playfully. "You know last time wasn't a full moon and it was a safe day to cum inside you but today is a different story."

Her eyes widen at realization as she squirms beneath me. "It's a full moon, darling. Anything can happen," I tease her as it sinks in. "Where do you want me to cum and you better decide quickly?"

Leah Silverwhisp

"A-are you saying that k-knotting is going to happen and—" her mind is clearly spinning as she slowly comes to terms with this.

"Yes, and yes," I confirm as I continue to pound into her.

She gasps loudly unable to answer me as my cock throbs as it begins to knot up inside her. Too late. I did warn her. I continue to pound into her going deep and hard until I finally release inside of her causing her to orgasm again. I roll over onto my back breathing heavily as I hear her panting beside me.

Haili forces herself up and bites down on my shoulder hard. I feel her teeth sink in, then she says, "I can't believe you used my love for pancakes against me."

"I love how that is your first reaction and not the fact that I just got you pregnant," I tease.

"I swear I will bite you again, Shev," she teases back.

167

"I can't tell which you like more being the biter or getting bitten," I tease her as I admire my handiwork. Her body is covered in my bite marks.

She bites my shoulder again. "So, now what?"

"Move in," I say, pulling her on top of me and kissing her deeply. "With me."

Haili returns the kiss and thinks for a moment. "You still owe me a date."

"Pancake punishment doesn't count?" I joke.

She bites my bottom lip. "Of course not, you owe me a whole day of just us that doesn't involve pancake punishment."

"Does helping you move in count as a date?" I tease playfully.

"Only if you stop procrastinating and actually start unpacking your things first," she says, trying to get up, but I hold her in place.

"Say it," I tease. "Say it or I'll keep you in the bedroom until you do."

Leah Silverwhisp

She rolls her eyes. "I'll move in with you, but after you unpack everything, and you take me on at least ten dates."

"Deal," I say, kissing her deeply and letting her go so she can get dressed.

The next couple of days, Haili and I start unpacking the rest of my stuff. She finds the copies of the books I bought for her with my own little annotations in them. I catch her reading all my little notes, her face turning red. I grin as I continue to unpack the last bit of my things, while saving the boxes to move her next things. Unfortunately, helping me unpack does not count as a date because of the whole pancake incident. Therefore, I plan to sweep her away tomorrow and take her to the bookstore where her best friend Ash works and buy her a new belt since I still haven't replaced her old one. Then figure out what I am doing for the next eight dates after that. On the tenth date, I already know.

When the tenth date finally comes, I stand nervously in front of my purple jeep wearing a suit and tie. Not my usual attire, but this is

Leah Silverwhisp

a very special occasion. I watch Haili step out of her parents' house and walk over to me in a cute little black dress with black sandals and a denim jacket. I take her hand and help her into the jeep.

"Why the jacket?" I ask curiously.

"Somebody had to leave bite marks all over me every time I came over to help them unpack," she teases.

I grin and hop into the driver's side. "Good point. I guess I'll have to hide my bite marks better then."

Her face flushes as I drive her to the parking lot of the mountains where she first shifted. I park the jeep and get out, walking around to the other side of the jeep. She opens the door, and I help her down and take her hand leading her to a picnic area where a blanket has been laid out with a basket of food that was prepped by Owen and an orchestra in the background playing phantom of the opera in the background.

Haili's free hand covers her mouth as she takes it all in. Fairy lights hang from the

Leah Silverwhisp

trees and a couple of books are stacked over by a nearby tent. She walks over to the blanket and picks up one of the books. Then the next one and the one after that.

She looks back over to me. "You bought the whole pack a copy of my book."

"Yup, and Selene wants to collab with you during her book month," I say and pick up the book on top of the wicker basket. "And this is mine." I pass the book over to her with a purple pen. "Can you sign mine with *will you marry me?* And a little heart."

I get on one knee as I pull out a bookmark with a ring attached to it. Haili starts to write it as she pauses in realization and looks over at me. The book and pen fall out of her hands. She nods unable to speak as I stand up and place the ring on her finger. Her lips find mine as I pull her close. Haili pulls back for a moment. "Yes," she says. "My answer is yes, and I will write it in your book later."

I chuckle and pull her closer to me. "I love you, Haili. I love every facial expression, every creative spark, every time you write, every moment I spend with you, and

Leah Silverwhisp

everything else. You are so amazingly bright and funny. I'm just so lucky that you are my mate."

"I love you too, Shev. Every soul connection, every tease, every gesture, and support you have given me. I love your wit, your playful sense of humor, and big heart. Every time we are together, I know my walls stand no chance with you."

I chuckle and kiss her deeply. "I told you I would lay siege to your timid castle."

Leah Silverwhisp

Leah Silverwhisp

P.S. Still here?

You've officially reached the end. The words are gone. The dragons are napping. The pancakes have been devoured. And me? I have a pack of spicy wolves whispering inside of my head to write more.

If you laughed, cried, or side-eyed a character lovingly, please consider leaving a review—it helps a witch out more than you know.

And if you dare reread, I won't stop you. Just watch out that you too don't get any bite marks.

Stay spellbound,
Leah Silverwhisp

Leah Silverwhisp

www.ingramcontent.com/pod-product-compliance
Lightning Source LLC
Chambersburg PA
CBHW030431120726
47903CB00003B/906